# FOOD IRRADIATION

## WHO WANTS IT?

# FOOD IRRADIATION

## WHO WANTS IT?

Tony Webb, Tim Lang, and Kathleen Tucker

With a forward by Michael Jacobson, Director
Center for Science in the Public Interest

Thorsons Publishers, Inc.
Rochester, Vermont
Wellingborough, Northamptonshire

First published in Great Britain under the title Food Irradiation: The
Facts by Thorsons Publishing Group, Wellingborough,
Northhamptonshire, 1987.

Library of Congress Cataloging-in-Publication Data
Webb, Tony
    Food irradiation.

    Bibliography: p.
    Includes index.
    1. Food, Irradiated.    2. Radiation preservation of
food. I. Lang, Tim.   II. Tucker, Kathleen.   III. Title.
TX571.R3W43   1987        363.1'92        87-10118
ISBN 0-7225-1071-3

Printed and bound in the United States

10 9 8 7 6 5 4 3

Distributed to the book trade in the United States by Harper and Row

Distributed to the book trade in Canada by Book Center, Inc., Montreal,
Quebec

Distributed to the health food trade in Canada by Alive Books, Toronto
and Vancouver

Distributed to the book trade outside the United States and Canada by
Thorsons Publishing Group, Wellingborough, Northamptonshire, England

# CONTENTS

# LIST OF TABLES AND FIGURES

# ACKNOWLEDGMENTS

No book is ever written by the authors alone. This book has been a genuinely international effort of authors both sides of the Atlantic and a big network of informants and experts around the world. *Food Irradiation* is an illustration of how food matters demonstrate global interdependence. We thank all who have given us advice, facts, and enthusiasm to delve into what has become a deep issue.

Special thanks must go in the United States to Bob Alvarez, Wally Burnstein, Catherine Frompovich, Michael Jacobson and all at the Center for Science in the Public Interest, Ayn Lowry, Denis Mosgofian, Keith Schaeffer, Connie Wheeler, Sid Wolfe, and our editor Leslie Colket; and in Canada, Linda Pim, David Poch, and Rosalie Bertell.

In the United Kingdom, we thank Liz Castledine, Claire-Marie Fortin, Melanie Hare, all the staff at the London Food Commission, the London Food Commission Food Irradiation Working Party, the Food Irradiation Campaign volunteers, and Fay Franklin and Judith Smallwood at Thorsons Publishing Group.

# GLOSSARY

ACINF: Advisory Committee on Irradiated and Novel Foods

AFL/CIO: American Federation of Labor and Congress of Industrial Organizations

BARC: Bhaba Atomic Research Centre (India)

BEUC: Bureau European des Unions de Consommateurs

CAIR: Citizens Against Irradiated Food (US)

CANAH: Coalition for Alternatives in Nutrition and Healthcare (US)

Co 60: Cobalt 60: radioactive isotope for food irradiation

Cs 137: Cesium 137: radioactive isotope for food irradiation

COMA: Committee on Medical Aspects of Food Policy (DHSS) (UK)

CUFFS: Consumers United for Food Safety

DHSS: Department of Health and Social Security (UK)

DOE: Department of Energy

ECF-IUF: European Committee of Food Catering and Allied Workers Unions within the International Union of Food Workers

EEC: European Economic Community

EHO: Environmental Health Officer (UK)

EIS: Environmental Impact Statement (US)

FAO: Food and Agriculture Organization (United Nations)

FAST: Food and Allied Services Trades Department of the AFL/CIO

FDA: Food and Drug Administration (US)

FDF: Food and Drink Federation (UK)

FIR: Food Irradiation Response (US)

FIRA: Food Industries Research Association (at Leatherhead, Surrey) (UK)

Gy: Gray: unit of received dose of radiation

HEI: Health and Energy Institute, Washington, DC

HHS: US Government Department of Health and Human Services

IAEA: International Atomic Energy Agency

IBT: Industrial Bio-Test Ltd.

ICRP: International Commission on Radiological Protection

IOCU: International Organisation of Consumers Unions

JECFI: Joint Expert Committee of the IAEA/WHO/FAO

kGy: kiloGray

LFC: London Food Commission (UK)

MEP: Member of the European Parliament

MP: Member of Parliament (UK)

mSv: milliSievert (see Sievert, below)

NACNE: National Advisory Committee for Nutrition Education (UK)

NCSFI: National Coalition to Stop Food Irradiation (US)

NIN: National Institute of Nutrition (Hyderabad, India)

OMB: Office of Management and Budget (US)

PA: Pubic Analysts (UK)

PUFA: Polyunsaturated Fatty Acid

Rad: old unit of received dose of radiation

Radurization: use of "low" doses (below 100,000 rad) (1 kGy)

Radicidation: use of "medium" doses (100,000-1 million rad) (1-10 kGy)

Raddapertization: use of higher doses (above 1 million rad) (10 kGy)

RDA: Recommended Daily Allowance (for vitamins)

rem: unit of dose measuring biological damage

Sv: Sievert: new unit of dose measuring biological damage done in living tissue

UK: United Kingdom

UN: United Nations

US: United States

USDA: United States Department of Agriculture

VAPOF: Vermont Alliance to Protect our Food

VPIRG: Vermont Public Interest Research Group

WHO: World Health Organization (of the United Nations)

# CHRONOLOGY

1916   Sweden experiments with irradiation of strawberries.

1921   Patents taken out in US.

1930   Patents taken out in France.

1953   Food irradiation to be one of the "atoms for peace" technologies; US Army begins research.

1957   Irradiation used on spices in West Germany.

1958   Food irradiation banned in West Germany.
USSR permits irradiation of potatoes.
US: Irradiation classed as an additive; safety testing required.

1960   Canada permits irradiation of potatoes.

1963   US permits irradiation of wheat, potatoes, and bacon.

1968   US FDA withdraws permit for bacon.
US Army studies found to indicate adverse effects and to have been poorly conducted.

1970s   Research program taken over by IBT Ltd.
IAEA organizes "expert seminars" and publishes reports on food irradiation.
IAEA sets up joint expert committee with WHO and FAO (JECFI).

1976   JECFI relaxes requirement for testing of irradiated foods so that radiolyte products do not have to pass tests normally required for food additives. Further permits for foods given by various countries.

1981   JECFI gives general clearance up to 1 million rad (10 kGy) (average dose) and removes requirement for control of maximum and minimum doses.
UN Codex Alimentarius process initiated.
Permits extended by various countries.
US FDA publishes proposals for fruits, vegetables, spices, and pork.

1982   UK Government ACINF set up to review evidence on safety and wholesomeness.
Codex Alimentarius Commission adopts JECFI proposals for general clearance up to 1 million rad (10 kGy).

1983   IBT officials convicted of doing fraudulent research for government and industry. US loses $4 million and 6 years of research data.

1984   US FDA publishes proposals to eliminate labeling of irradiated foods.

1985    US DOE proposes spending $10 million to build six demonstration irradiation plants. Offers cesium 137 at one-tenth of market price of cobalt 60.
US FDA gives clearance to irradiation of pork for control of trichinae.

1986    Scandal over abuse of irradiation by British food companies illegally concealing bacterial contamination on imports to UK and Sweden.
US approves clearance of irradiation for fruit and vegetables up to 100,000 rad (1 kGy) and 3 million rad (30 kGy) for spices.
UK ACINF report published: recommends there are no special safety problems from irradiation of food up to 10 kGy.

1987    European Parliament votes against general approval of irradiation for European Community "on precautionary grounds" and instructs the European Commission to investigate alternative methods of preservation for those EEC countries that have approved it.
Canadian Parliament Standing Committee calls for more research before irradiation is widely used, and recommends that wheat irradiation no longer be permitted.

# INTRODUCTION

Irradiation. The very word is a bit scary, conjuring up images of Hiroshima and Chernobyl, x-rays and cancer. Despite its widespread medical uses, irradiation is inherently hazardous and therefore a source of great concern.

For most consumers, irradiation of foods has been an issue of theoretical, not practical, significance. But that's about to change. The nuclear industry and segments of the food industry, with assistance from government agencies, recently gained permission to preserve a wide variety of foods with irradiation. So while right now a small part of your dinner might have been bombarded with gamma rays, in the next few years hundreds of foods may be treated.

Zealous proponents paint an attractive picture of the glories of irradiation: more abundant food supplies, reduced use of dangerous pesticides, fewer hungry people, lower prices. Equally zealous opponents with health and environmental concerns paint a far grimmer picture: dangerous new chemicals in food, greater cancer risk, rotten food magically made "fresh."

While the "experts" bandy about such terms as kiloGrays, cobalt 60, and radappertization, the average consumer is left more confused than enlightened. Tony Webb and Tim Lang, of the London (England) Food Commission, and Kathleen Tucker, of the Washington, DC-based Health and Energy Institute (both non-profit organizations), have written this book for concerned citizens who want to understand both sides of the argument better.

The irradiation industry contends that "hundreds of studies" prove irradiation to be a safe and beneficial process. The closer one gets to those studies, though, the less persuasive they look. The Food and Drug Administration, which has approved irradiation of many foods, has faulted a number of the studies because they were poorly designed or performed by untrustworthy laboratories. The agency has cited five studies in support of its approval of irradiation, but it doesn't claim that this handful of studies can be considered decisive—and it hasn't satisfactorily addressed several studies that did show adverse effects.

The primary consumer safety issue revolves around the new chemical compounds—unique radiolytic products (URP)—produced in foods by irradiation, and whether some of these substances are harmful. Ideally, each new substance would be isolated, identified, and fed in large quantity to laboratory animals, or otherwise tested to determine if it can cause mutations, cancer, liver damage, immunological deficiencies, or other problems. But such tests would be extremely expensive and time-consuming, and they will probably never be conducted. In the absence of those tests, the FDA says that, judging from known radiolytic products, none of the chemicals produced by irradiation is likely to be harmful. Furthermore, even if they were harmful in large amounts, the minuscule levels produced in food would pose no risk to consumers.

Many consumers who don't feel their doubts have been satisfied would prefer to avoid treated food. But will they be able to? The FDA says, "sort of—at least for a while." The law requires that irradiated foods be labeled with identifying wording ("treated with irradiation") and a flower-like symbol only until 1988. At that time the wording requirement will expire, although the FDA may extend it. Furthermore, labeling is required only when the entire food has been treated. So, for example, vegetable soup containing irradiated potatoes would be exempt. Moreover, restaurants and cafeterias do not have to disclose the use of irradiation, just as they do not now disclose the use of dyes, preservatives, and other additives.

Another troubling point the authors raise is that it is impossible to determine whether a food has been irradiated, or at what dose. Consequently, government inspectors cannot verify that dosages have been kept to safe and legal levels. Conversely, when a manufacturer claims to have preserved its products with irradiation, there is no way to confirm this. The authors argue that, safety aside, irradiation should not be permitted until such detection and verification methods have been developed.

While most of the public discussion has focused on the danger of radiolytic products to consumers, the authors identify other possible hazards:

- To what extent does irradiation affect vitamin content?
- Would unscrupulous processors use irradiation to reduce or destroy bacteria in substandard, decaying foods, and then sell these foods as though they were fresh, high quality products? (This illegal activity has already occurred in Europe.)
- Might workers in irradiation facilities inadvertently be exposed to dangerous levels of radioactive materials?
- Would radioactive materials be dispersed accidentally through the environment?

It is questions like these that have made many people nervous about the whole technology. And in response to that nervousness, executives of a number of supermarket chains and manufacturing firms have said they will not market irradiated foods until consumers' concerns have been more adequately satisfied.

The issue of irradiation is but one of many food safety problems that clamor for the public's attention. Top government and industry officials sanctimoniously claim that Americans enjoy "the world's safest food supply." But lower-level officials and scientists acknowledge numerous, serious problems. The Center for Disease Control, for instance, estimates that food poisoning, caused by *Salmonella, Campylobacter*, and other bacteria, kills about 9,000 Americans a year and causes tens of millions of illnesses. The FDA has acknowledged that farmers and veterinarians are illegally using vast numbers of drugs on livestock. And certain legal animal drugs—antibiotics—are undermining the value of antibiotics as medicines for people. Plant foods are not necessarily pure, because most are contaminated with residues of one or more pesticides, and some contain illegally high levels. Finally, of course, are the food additives that can cause everything from headaches to asthmatic attacks to cancer in susceptible individuals: MSG, sulfite, sodium nitrite, saccharin, and others. Even without irradiation, our dinner plate is chock-full of question marks.

To help make our food supply truly the world's safest, the Center for Science in the Public Interest, in coalition with other national and local organizations, is sponsoring the Americans for Safe Food project (P.O. Box 66300, Washington, DC 20035). Americans for Safe

Food is a broad-based effort that is harnessing the energies of consumers, environmentalists, organic farmers, and others to increase the availability of uncontaminated food: food grown and processed without pesticides, chemical additives, drugs . . . and irradiation. If the market demands such food, eventually the producers will supply it. And as long as foods are treated with pesticides, other chemicals, or irradiation, labels or shelf markers should clearly say so.

The irradiation controversy will certainly intensify in the coming years if the government approves more uses and if industry invests in new plants. It is not only food that is at issue, but also the development of a new nuclear industry that would make radioactive materials—with their inherent dangers—increasingly a part of our everyday lives. Fortunately, though, few foods are now being irradiated, and no large industry is unilaterally determining national policies. There is time for considered debate and, where appropriate, more scientific research. And with that time, citizens have an opportunity to develop their own position on whether to take or leave irradiated food—or, indeed, whether food irradiation and the technology that surrounds it should be stopped altogether.

Michael F. Jacobson, Ph.D.
Executive Director
Center for Science in the Public Interest
Washington, DC

# CHAPTER 1

# THE BEST THING SINCE SLICED BREAD?

WE ALL NEED to eat. The recent support for famine aid projects shows that we are concerned for those who do not have enough food, or not enough of the right kind. Among those of us who have enough, there is also concern over the quality of the food we eat.

We want good fresh food with fewer additives and pesticide residues. At the same time, we want to be able to eat what we like, when and where we like. We have come to expect seafood in the Midwest, fresh fruit in the middle of winter. We often want food that can be quickly turned into an attractive meal. In short, we want quality and convenience.

The food industries have used a variety of methods over the years to both encourage and meet the demand for convenience. As well as processing food to simplify the task of preparation and cooking, considerable effort has gone into developing techniques to preserve or extend the shelf life of food. These techniques have included cooking, salting, drying, bottling, canning, packaging, smoking, chilling, freezing, dehydrating, and using chemical additives. The main aim has been to extend the time that food can remain in storage, in transport, or in the stores before it is sold to the customer, and the time he or she can keep it at home before it goes "bad."

We have, in fact, been remarkably successful in doing this. As a result, the developed world now enjoys, literally, the fruits of the earth, and access to just about every food available anywhere on the globe. We have, however, been less successful in sharing these benefits with the less well-developed countries. Apart from extreme cases of famine and drought, the problem of hunger is not one of shortage but of a failure to distribute the food to those in need. Much of this is undoubtedly due to economic factors. We can afford their food; they cannot. But, equally, we cannot be blind to the fact that some 25 to 30% of the food in many areas is wasted for lack of the ability to harvest, store, and transport it to where it is needed. Any additional technology that adds to our ability to preserve food deserves consideration.

However, each of the preservation techniques has a price—both an economic one and a price in terms of the damage it does to the quality of the food. Processing and storage inevitably result in some loss of nutrients and the traces of vitamins that are needed to maintain health. Freezing may damage the texture of foods. Even cooking causes some effects that are undesirable from a health standpoint, even though it makes many foods edible. No system for preserving food is 100% perfect.

It is also being recognized that some techniques are less perfect than others. The growing concern over chemical additives has, in many instances, a solid foundation. Many additives are not used for preservation but for cosmetic or economic reasons, making the food look attractive but disguising a lack of nutritional value. A number of those officially approved as "safe" have been shown to be hazardous to human health. Others cause acute reactions in particular individuals that suggest a cause for concern, not just for the susceptible group but perhaps for the whole population. Workers who handle these chemicals in much larger quantities than those consumed by the public can and do suffer health damage from breathing and handling these additives. These workers are, in a very real sense, the guinea pigs on whom we can observe just how hazardous some of the additives are. Many of the studies in which such chemicals were safety-tested on animals have been found to be poorly conducted or, in some cases, downright fraudulent.

The demand for high-quality food has expanded far beyond the "health food" lobby where it began. It goes beyond those who can afford to buy into alternative lifestyles. It is being reflected in the policies of leading supermarket chains that now insist their suppliers provide additive-free alternatives to many common processed goods. Public school boards have set standards for their suppliers in order to provide a more healthy diet for school pupils. National governments are advocating gradual but significant dietary change as a way of combating some of the killer diseases of our age. All of this is changing the face of the food industry and the expectations we have of food and a balanced diet.

It is in this context that we consider the development of the latest in this long line of food processing technologies—irradiation. This process involves using very large doses of ionizing radiation, which, it is claimed, will inhibit the sprouting of vegetables; delay the ripening of fruits; kill insect pests in fruit, grains, or spices; kill or render sterile parasites such as trichinae in pork; reduce or eliminate the microorganisms that cause food to spoil; and in particular reduce the bacteria such as *Salmonella* on some meats and seafood products that cause food poisoning. It has been hailed as an alternative to other methods of preservation, such as the use of chemical additives. It is claimed that the process is completely safe and that consumers will benefit from reduced wastage, greater convenience, and better quality food.

Many of these uses are attractive. Pesticides and fumigation treatments of fruit are now recognized as being hazardous to the workers who use them. Food poisoning outbreaks are increasing, and anything that may help reduce food losses in third world countries clearly should be considered.

Against this view, there is a body of opinion that points to a variety of adverse effects from irradiation, such as unique chemical changes, loss of vitamins, unpleasant flavors and odors, a limited range of foods for which the process has been found suitable, the necessity for use of additives to offset undesirable effects, and studies showing adverse health effects in animals and humans fed with irradiated foods.

Concern has been expressed within labor unions over possible health effects on members working in irradiation plants, and by environmental groups over the transport of radioactive material and discharge of radioactive effluent at the local community level. Such critics point to violations of worker and public safety regulations that have occurred in irradiation plants in the United States and to the inadequacy of United States and international regulations on radiation protection.

Consumer groups have expressed concern over labeling of irradiated foods. At the very least, they believe that the consumer has a right to know if any food or ingredient of processed foods has been irradiated. Irradiated foods look fresh and retain the appearance of freshness longer. Without labeling, the possibility of counterfeit "freshness" can be easily exploited.

Such concerns are reinforced by evidence of significant nutritional losses in irradiated foods, especially the severe damage to some vitamins and to essential polyunsaturated fats and fatty acids. It is now widely recognized that there must be a change in the public diet. The very foods that the nutritional consensus now recommends increased consumption of—white meats, whole grains, fresh fruits, and vegetables—are the foods targeted for irradiation and in which significant nutrient losses will occur. Nutritionists are worried that use of irradiation will undermine the recent progress in promoting dietary change.

Not all sectors of the food industry want irradiation. Some are worried about the possibility of its introduction, others are concerned about additional regulation in the food trade that may be needed if it is introduced, and many are worried about consumer reaction and are hedging their bets. Some importers and retailers in Europe have spoken out strongly against it, sometimes out of self-interest, but often for more principled reasons.

There is also evidence from Europe that some food suppliers have used the process to eliminate high bacterial loads on food in order to make them saleable. Besides being illegal, this practice is in violation of recommendations of the World Health Organization, and could in some cases lead to serious health hazards. Irradiation may reduce the bacterial load on food, however, it does not eliminate the chemical toxins that may have been created by earlier contamination.

At present there is no test that can be used by any nation's health agencies to detect irradiation. It will be several years before a suitable test of this kind is developed, and even longer before tests are developed that will enable us to tell if food has been re-irradiated and, if so, how many times and with what doses.

Despite this, the United States government agencies, the Food and Drug Administration (FDA) and the Department of Agriculture (USDA), have progressively permitted the use of irradiation on an ever widening range of foods. They have, it has to be said, moved more cautiously than several other countries. Even so, several European countries, notably Britain, West Germany, and most of the Scandinavian countries, retain a strict ban on the irradiation and importation of any irradiated foods for human consumption.

Consumers' groups in some third world countries suggest that irradiation may not be an appropriate technology to prevent food wastage and that many measures, often simpler ones, are needed before irradiation is considered.

There is considerable emotional reaction to the term "irradiation." Some sectors of the industry fear that this will lead to unreasonable consumer resistance to irradiated foods. In some countries there have been moves to ban the use of the term "irradiated" and to substitute less emotive symbols or words for labeling purposes. Consumer organizations everywhere are united in their insistence that all food must be clearly labeled as "irradiated," thus ensuring that consumers have the opportunity to choose between irradiated and nonirradiated foods. The labeling of loose fruit and vegetables and of food sold in restaurants will pose enormous enforcement problems.

Look at it this way. If you were trying to sell irradiated fruit and vegetables and your customers wouldn't buy it, would you label it knowing that no one could prove it was irradiated? Or, to put it another way, if irradiation were widely accepted and welcomed by consumers, what would stop you from claiming that the food you were selling had been irradiated? The whole system is wide open to counterfeiting based on the way irradiated foods may appear fresh for longer.

The facts about food irradiation go beyond the pure sciences of toxicology, microbiology, and nutrition (which are discussed later in this book). They extend also to issues of concern about irradiation in the real world. In the real world of food supply and consumption, money and cost influence decisions about what is acceptable. What financial benefits are to be had? More importantly, by whom? It hardly inspires public confidence to discover that some who stand to gain most have been intimately involved in promoting the benefits of the technology, and that their own companies have benefited from speculation that the government agencies are about to remove bans or permit extensions to the use of irradiation.

If irradiation of food is to be allowed, then we need to be sure that it will bring real benefits to consumers. We need to be sure either that there are no risks or that risks to the public and to those who work in the food industries are reduced to a minimum by effective regulations. We will also need an effective system for enforcing these regulations that can prevent abuses.

In this book we will examine the facts about the safety and wholesomeness of irradiated food and whether the technology is both controllable and needed. These issues will be examined from the standpoint of the United States and also from an international perspective. The market for food is increasingly international, and there are considerable pressures to have a common standard among all countries that will allow unrestricted trade in irradiated foods. This will open the United States to uses of irradiation that are currently not permitted, and require countries that currently ban the process to permit it.

Supporters of food irradiation have argued that the process has the endorsement of such eminent bodies as the World Health Organization, and that it has been granted permits in some 30 countries; yet, as we shall discover, the assurances appear to be based more on accumulated opinion carefully fostered by some interests that appear to have more to do with the nuclear industries than with the food industry. These opinions are far from convincingly supported by the facts.

We are not opposed to food irradiation. However critical we may appear to be, we accept that there may be benefits in the use of new processing technologies. What we object to is the way that it is being promoted with arguments that are totally one-sided and that ignore legitimate concerns that need to be addressed. The time has come to reexamine the case for and against food irradiation. This examination should have taken place before we reached this stage. At the very least it must take place now. We need to examine the facts, and then, armed with these facts, the American public needs to enter the debate about whether the process should be allowed to continue, expand, or be halted. This must be an informed public debate, not, as until now, one dominated by scientists, public officials, and those in the food and nuclear industries who stand to benefit.

## A Brief History of Food Irradiation

The idea of irradiating food is not new. We have had nearly 70 years of experimentation with it. The treatment was tested on strawberries in Sweden in 1916. The first patents on the idea were taken out in the United States in 1921, and in France in 1930. Little progress was made, however, until 1953, when President Eisenhower announced the "Atoms for Peace Program." Public attention was to be shifted away from nuclear weapons by the promotion of nuclear power and other uses of nuclear technology, so that the academic and industrial infrastructure could be developed behind which the weapons program would continue. There followed a decade of intensive research into food irradiation, funded and supervised by the United States Department of Defense.[1,2]

The first commercial use of food irradiation actually occured in West Germany in 1957, for the sterilization of spices used in the manufacture of sausage. This was brought to an abrupt end when the German government banned the process in 1958. The Soviet Union was the first government to permit irradiation, for inhibiting the sprouting of potatoes in 1958, and for disinfestation of grain in 1959. Canada permitted its use for potatoes in 1960. The United States Food, Drug, and Cosmetics Act of 1958 defined the irradiation process as an additive. Users have to petition the Food and Drug Administration for permission to market irradiated products. This has resulted in stringent requirements for testing of irradiated foods in the United States. Not until 1963 was clearance given for sterilization of can-packed bacon and the inhibition of potato sprouting and wheat disinfestation already in use elsewhere. The FDA, however, rescinded the bacon approval in 1968, citing possible health problems with the test animals and deficiencies in the way some experiments were designed and conducted.[3] A list of regulatory permits in the United States is given in Table 1.

About 30 countries have permitted irradiation of 28 different foods for public consumption (Table 2). Commercial activities were planned in a further 11 countries as of January 1985.[4]

There are some notable exceptions. Britain, West Germany, and most of the Scandinavian countries currently do not permit irradiation of food for public consumption.[5] So far, in Britain, permission has been given only for animal feed, and for irradiation of food for hospital patients needing sterile diets. This may soon change as a result of the report of the British government's Advisory Committee on Irradiated and Novel Foods,[6] and with the growing pressures for harmonization of national legislation within the countries of the European Economic Community.[7]

Although several countries have given permits for food irradiation, there has been little use of the technology. Eighteen countries actually

## Table 1: US Regulatory Permits for Irradiation of Foods

| Date Approved | Petition for | Maximum Dose | Petitioner |
|---|---|---|---|
| 8/63 | Insect disinfestation of wheat and wheat flour | 50,000 rad (0.5 kGy) | Atomic Energy Commission |
| 10/64 | Sprout inhibition of potatoes | 15,000 rad (0.15 kGy) | Univ. of Michigan |
| 7/83 | Insect and microbiological control in onion powder, garlic powder, and spices | 1,000,000 rad (10 kGy) | Radiation Tech, Inc. |
| 6/85 | Dry powdery and immobilized enzyme preparations | 1,000,000 rad (10 kGy) | Radiation Tech, Inc. |
| 7/85 | Pork products to control trichinae | 100,000 rad (1 kGy) | Radiation Tech, Inc. |
| 4/86 | Fruits and vegetables for insect disinfestation | 100,000 rad (1 kGy) | FDA |
| 4/86 | Herbs, spice blends, and vegetable seasonings | 3,000,000 rad (30 kGy) | FDA |

(Source: Health and Energy Institute.)

engage in irradiation, but the scale of its use is still very small. As well as worries about consumer reactions, the mixture of protective and permissive national regulations clearly acts as a barrier to international trade in irradiated food products, which food manufacturers would like to see removed.

The International Atomic Energy Agency (IAEA), the World Health Organization (WHO), and the Food and Agriculture Organization (FAO) of the United Nations have collaborated on a joint initiative to research and promote food irradiation since the early 1960s. These organizations have funded an international Food Irradiation Research Project at Karlsruhe in West Germany since 1970, and a joint IAEA/WHO/FAO committee produced key reports in 1976[8] and 1980[9] on the wholesomeness of irradiated foods. At the same time, the Codex Alimentarius Committee of the United Nations (UN) has formulated

## Table 2: Foods Given Permits for Irradiation by Country*

| Foods | Argentina | Australia | Bangladesh | Belgium | Brazil | Canada | Chile | China | Denmark | France | German Democratic Republic | Hungary | Israel | Italy | Japan | The Netherlands | New Zealand | Norway | Philippines | Poland | South Africa | Spain | Thailand | Uruguay | US** | USSR | Yugoslavia |
|---|---|---|---|---|---|---|---|---|---|---|---|---|---|---|---|---|---|---|---|---|---|---|---|---|---|---|---|
| Potatoes | × | | × | × | × | × | × | × | × | × | | | × | × | × | × | | | × | × | × | × | | × | × | × | × |
| Onions | | | × | × | × | × | × | × | | × | | | × | × | | × | | | × | × | × | × | | | × | × | × |
| Garlic | | | | × | | | | × | | × | × | | × | × | | | | | × | | × | | × | | | | × |
| Shallots | | | | × | | | | | | × | | | × | | | | | | | | | | | | | | |
| Wheat & other grains | | | × | | × | × | × | × | | | | | | | | × | | | | | | | | | | × | |
| Spices | | | × | | × | × | × | | | × | × | × | × | | | × | × | × | | | | | | | × | | |
| Chicken | | | × | | | | × | | | | | × | × | | | × | | | | | | | | | × | | |
| Fish (incl. frozen) | | × | × | | × | | × | | | | | | | | | × | | | | | × | | | | | | |
| Frozen shrimps | | | × | | | | | | | | | | | | | × | | | | | × | | | | | | |
| Boiled shrimps | | | | | | | | | | | | | | | | × | | | | | | | | | | | |
| Frog legs (incl. frozen) | | | × | | | | | | | | | | | | | × | | | | | | | | | | | |
| Rye bread | | | | | | | | | | | | | | | | × | | | | | | | | | | | |
| Egg powder | | | | | | | | | | | | | | | | × | | | | | | | | | | | × |
| Blood proteins | | | | | | | | | | | | | | | | × | | | | | | | | | | | |
| Cocoa beans | | | | | | × | | | | | | | | | | × | | | | | | | | | | | |
| Dates | | | | | | × | | | | | | | | | | × | | | | | | | | | | | |
| Pulses | | | | | | × | | | | | | | | | | × | | | | | | | | | | | |

*continued*

## Table 2 continued

| Foods | Argentina | Australia | Bangladesh | Belgium | Brazil | Canada | Chile | China | Denmark | France | German Democratic Republic | Hungary | Israel | Italy | Japan | The Netherlands | New Zealand | Norway | Philippines | Poland | South Africa | Spain | Thailand | Uruguay | US** | USSR | Yugoslavia |
|---|---|---|---|---|---|---|---|---|---|---|---|---|---|---|---|---|---|---|---|---|---|---|---|---|---|---|---|
| Pawpaw (papaya) | | | X | | X | | X | | | | | | | | | | | | | | X | | | | | | |
| Mango (incl. pickled) | | | X | | | | X | | | | | | | | | | | | | | X | | | | | | |
| Strawberries | | | | X | X | | X | | | | | | | | | X | | | | | X | | | | | | |
| Paprika | | | | X | | | | | | | | | | | | | | | | | | | | | | | |
| Mangoachar | | | | | | | | | | | | | | | | | | | | | | | | | | | |
| Bananas (incl. dried) | | | | | | | | | | | | | | | | | | | | | X | | | | | | |
| Dry food concentrate | | | | | | | | | | | | | | | | | | | | | X | | | | | X | |
| Dried fruits | | | | | | | | | | | | | | | | | | | | | | | | | X | X | |
| Mushrooms | | | | | | | | X | | | | | | | | X | | | | | | | | | | | |
| Endive | | | | | | | | | | | | | | | | X | | | | | | | | | | | |
| Asparagus | | | | | | | | | | | | | | | | X | | | | | | | | | | | |
| Batter mix | | | | | | | | | | | | | | | | X | | | | | | | | | | | |
| Wheat flour | | | X | | X | X | X | | | | | | | | | X | | | | | | | | | X | | |
| Rice & rice products | | | X | | X | X | X | | | | | | | | | | | | | | | | | | | | |
| Gum arabic | | | | X | | | | | | | | | | | | | | | | | | | | | | | |
| Dried vegetables | | | | X | | | | | | X | | | | | | X | | | | | X | | | | | | X |
| Fish products | | | | | X | | X | | | | | | X | | | | | | | | | | | | | | |
| Poultry | | | | | X | | | | | X | | | | | | | | | | | | | | | | | |
| Peanuts | | | | | | | | X | | | | | | | | | | | | | | | | | | | X |
| Sausage | | | | | | | | X | | | | | | | | | | | | | | | | | | | |
| Malt | | | | | | | | | | | | | | | | X | | | | | | | | | | | |

| | |
|---|---|
| Herbs | ✗ |
| Pork, fresh | ✗ |
| Cereals | ✗ |
| Legumes | ✗ |
| Tea extracts | ✗ |
| Herbal tea | ✗ |
| Enzymes (incl. dried preps) | ✗ |
| Litchis | ✗ |
| Avocadoes | ✗ |
| Fruit juices (frozen) | ✗ |
| Green beans | ✗ |
| Tomatoes | ✗ |
| Brinjals | ✗ |
| Soya pickle products | ✗ |
| Ginger | ✗ |
| Vegetable paste | ✗ |
| Almonds | ✗ |
| Cheese powder | ✗ |
| Yeast powder | ✗ |

*This list includes unconditional and provisional clearances for commercial sale, but not clearances for experimental or test marketing trials.

**The US has given permission for all fruits and vegetables up to 100,000 rad (kGy).

(Source: Coalition for Alternatives in Nutrition & Healthcare, 1985.)

International Guidelines on irradiated foods based on the recommendations of this joint committee.[10] It has recommended that there are no special safety reasons why food should not be irradiated up to a dose of 1 million rad (10 kGy).

So far, the United States Food and Drug Administration has recommended that general irradiation be permitted only up to the lower dose of 100,000 rad (1 kGy)—one tenth of the Codex level. The exception to this is spices, which are to be permitted doses up to 3 million rad (30 kGy).[11,12] The USDA, which has control of the regulation of standards for processing of meats, particularly poultry and pork, has been slightly more restrictive, particularly over the use of vacuum packaging of meats, for reasons we will discuss later.

On the other hand, irradiation companies have been promoting the technology aggressively in the United States, and the Department of Energy (DOE) is preparing to finance demonstration irradiation plants and provide access to cheap sources of radioactive material as part of its nuclear waste management program.

Meanwhile, a coalition of interests has begun to emerge as opponents of food irradiation, not just in the United States but in Australia, New Zealand, Malaysia, Japan, and throughout Europe and Scandinavia. It has clearly become an issue of national and international concern, one where the facts on which to base responsible decisions are needed to counteract misinformation and unreasoned opinion on both sides. If and when irradiation takes its place beside other appropriate food processing technologies, we need to be assured that we are having only its real benefits and none of the unnecessary risks that come from over-hasty decision making at the behest of hidden interests.

REFERENCES

1. Edward S. Josephson and Martin S. Peterson, eds. *Preservation of Food by Ionizing Radiation* (3 vols.). Florida: CRC Press, Vol. 1 1982, Vols. 2 & 3 1983.
2. P. S. Elias and A. J. Cohen. *Recent Advances in Food Irradiation.* Amsterdam and New York: Elsevier Biomedical Press, 1983.

3. US Government Accounting Office. *The Department of the Army's Food Irradiation Program—Is It Worth Continuing?* PSAD-78-146 (September 29, 1978), pp. 6, 14; Spiher. "Food Irradiation: An FDA Report." *FDA Papers* (October 1968), p. 15.

4. US Agency for International Development. Draft Feasibility Study. Washington, DC, May 1985.

5. See Answer to Written Question No. 1398/81 by Mr. Narjes on 25 November 1982 to Mr. Schmid, and also Answer to Mrs. Hanna Walz, Question 1618/83, given 7 February 1984 in the European Parliament, Brussels.

6. *The Safety and Wholesomeness of Irradiated Foods.* Report of the Advisory Committee on Irradiated and Novel Foods. London: HMSO, 1986.

7. Lord Cockfield's Memorandum: Completion of the Internal Market, COM [85] 310; and Community Legislation on Foodstuffs, COM [85] 603. European Commission, Brussels, 1985.

8. World Health Organization. *Wholesomeness of Irradiated Food.* Report of Joint FAO/IAEA/WHO Expert Committee. WHO Technical Report Series No. 604, Geneva, 1977.

9. World Health Organization. *Wholesomeness of Irradiated Food.* Report of Joint FAO/IAEA/WHO Expert Committee. WHO Technical Report Series No. 659, Geneva, 1981.

10. Codex Alimentarius Commission. FAO/WHO, *Reports of the Executive Committee of the Codex Alimentarius Commission.* United Nations, Rome, 1978, 1981.

11. Department of Health and Human Services. Food and Drug Administration 21 CFR Part 179, Irradiation in the Production, Processing and Handling of Food; Final Rule. 51 Federal Register 13376 at 13385, Washington D.C., April 18, 1986.

12. Tony Webb and Tim Lang. *Food Irradiation: The Facts.* London: Thorsons, 1987.

# CHAPTER 2

# WHAT IS FOOD IRRADIATION?

VERY SIMPLY, FOOD irradiation is a treatment involving very large doses of ionizing radiation to produce some desired changes in food, particularly those allowing longer storage, or shelf life. This section covers the nature of radiation and what it does, the types of irradiation plants, radioactive sources used, the doses involved, and the question on everyone's mind: can food become radioactive?

## Ionizing Radiation

Radiation is a household word that covers a wide spectrum of energy. At the low end of the spectrum are the emissions from power lines and visual display units. Higher up are radiowaves and microwaves. Also included are infrared, visible, and ultraviolet light, and at the upper end are found x-rays, and gamma rays from radioactive material.

When radiation strikes other material it transfers its energy. This

**Figure 1. Radiation**

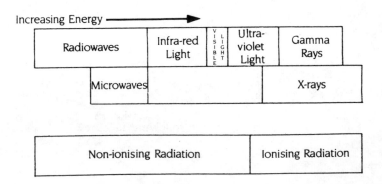

14

energy transfer can cause heating, as with microwave cooking or lying in the sunshine. At a certain level the radiation has sufficient energy to knock electrons out of the atoms of the material bombarded. This can break the molecular structure of the material, leaving positively and negatively charged particles called *ions* or *free radicals*. At or above this level the radiation is called ionizing radiation.[1] The ions are chemically very active and easily recombine or initiate chemical reactions with surrounding material.

Thus, ionizing radiation alters the chemical structure of material, which in turn can have biological effects on the behavior of living organisms and the materials they feed on.[2]

Some of the biological effects in the irradiation of food can be considered desirable. Irradiation of living organisms, especially people, is almost always damaging.[3,4,5]

## Food Irradiation Plants

In general, an irradiation plant consists of the following facilities:

1. A loading facility, where the food to be irradiated is packaged and pretreated by heating and/or refrigeration as needed and loaded onto conveyors that carry it to

2. The irradiation cell, where food is exposed to the radiation source. This can be either a cobalt or cesium gamma ray source, or an x-ray or electron beam machine source. The distance the food passes from the source and the length of time it is exposed determine the dose that the food receives. The size of the batch controls the extent to which the food is uniformly exposed or has large differences between maximum and minimum doses to different parts of the food batch. Thick concrete shielding protects workers from direct exposure to the source. It then passes into

3. A storage facility, where it is removed from the conveyor and stored at the required (usually low) temperatures before being sent to long-term storage or retailing outlets.

In addition, the plant needs the following facilities:

1. A fuel handling unit, where irradiated radioactive sources in the form of sealed rods or strips of cobalt 60 or cesium 137 are received and loaded by remote handling into the irradiator. They are usually

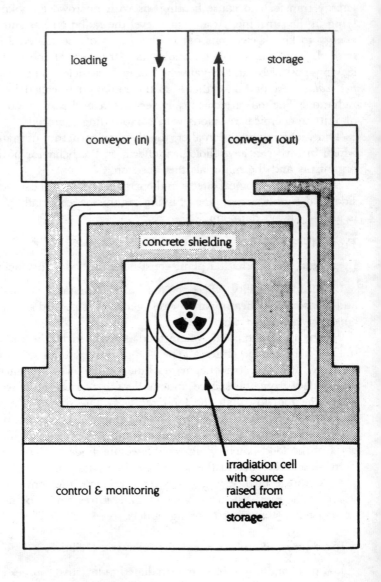

**Figure 2. Layout of an irradiation plant.**

stored under water, or in some instances in dry gas storage, and raised from them into the irradiation cell to expose the food.

2. A control unit, which governs the movement of the food (and the radioactive sources) through the irradiator.

3. There are also facilities for monitoring doses to the food and keeping records.

The design of the irradiation cell, the siting of the radioactive sources, and the path of the food through the cell depends on the type of food being irradiated. Some types of irradiator use a central source and pass the food around it on one of several circular tracks.

The arrangement of conveyor and source can be more complicated, with the food container turned so that it is irradiated from both sides. The aim is to achieve as small a difference as possible between the outside and the center of the bulk food package. In practice, however, these differences can be quite large unless the thickness of the bulk package is small.

Some foods such as fish may pass along a tube or between two parallel sources. The Atomic Energy Commission had a demonstration low-level irradiator for use on board ships, but the prototype took up too much space and was moved to a dock instead. If this idea is revived, the plan is to lightly irradiate fish at sea and then further irradiate them when they come ashore.

Other facilities may use a simple conveyor belt to carry food past either a gamma ray or a machine source of radiation. The French have designs for a small-scale field irradiator for potatoes. There are plans for a mobile irradiator to be mounted on a 40-foot truck.[6]

There are currently around 50 planned or operating irradiation facilities worldwide that are licensed to irradiate food,[6,7] 17 of which are currently operating in the United States (Table 3).[8,9] The major company involved is Isomedix, with seven plants and plans for three more. The Department of Energy proposes to build six demonstration irradiators in Hawaii, Washington, Alaska, Iowa, Oklahoma, and Florida.

In Europe, the main facilities are the Gammaster plant at Ede, The Netherlands, and the IRE plant at Fleurus, Belgium. Tables 4 and 5 indicate the other countries which have irradiation plants capable of irradiating food.[6] The Soviet Union is currently the largest

### Table 3: US Food Irradiators, Summer 1986

| Company | Location |
| --- | --- |
| Applied Radiant Energy Corp. | Lynchburg, Va. |
| International Nutronics | Irvine, Calif. |
| | Palo Alto, Calif. |
| Isomedix, Inc. | Columbus, Miss. |
| | Libertyville, Ill. |
| | Morton Grove, Ill. |
| | Northborough, Mass. |
| | Sandy, Utah |
| | Spartanburg, S.C. |
| | Vega Alta, Puerto Rico |
| Radiation Sterilizers, Inc. | Decatur, Ga. |
| | Fort Worth, Tex. |
| | Schaumburg, Ill. |
| | Tustin, Calif. |
| Radiation Technology | Rockaway, N.J. |
| | Haw River, N.C. |
| | West Memphis, Ark. |

(Source: Reference 8, 9.)

user of irradiation, almost exclusively for grain.

Although irradiation of food is still illegal in Britain, ten plants in Britain currently irradiate medical supplies or animal feed. Of these, only four, all owned by Isotron plc, will be able to handle commercial food irradiation. One other may be able to do so, and privatization of some hospital facilities may open possibilities for others on a small scale.[10,11]

A list of known gamma irradiation facilities in the United States is given in Appendix 1.[9] Several of those currently irradiating medical supplies may also be capable of irradiating food.

## Radioactive Food?

The first concern of most people is whether or not food becomes radioactive. Ionizing radiation with high energy can cause radio-activity to be created in the material that is bombarded.[1,3,5] The

### Table 4: Commercial Irradiators Available for Treating Food or Animal Feed (1986)

| Nation | Company (City) | Food Item (tons per year) | Starting Date |
|---|---|---|---|
| Belgium | IRE (Fleurus) | Spices (350 t/y) | 1981 |
| | | Dehydrated vegetables (700 t/y) | |
| | | Deep-frozen foods (2,000 t/y) | |
| Brazil | Embrarad (Sao Paulo) | Spices, dehydrated vegetables | 1985 |
| Chile | CCHEN (Santiago) | Onions (200–300 t/y) | 1983 |
| | | Potatoes (50–100 t/y) | |
| | | Spices & dehydrated vegetables (20–30 t/y) | |
| China | Nuclear Research Institute (Shanghai) | Potatoes | 1985 |
| Denmark | Riso National Laboratory | Spices | 1986 |
| Finland | Kolmi-Set Oy (Ilomantsi) | Spices | 1986 |
| France | Conservatome (Lyon) | Spices (500–600 t/y) | 1982 |
| | Caric (Paris) | Spices, poultry (300 t/y) | 1986 |
| German Democratic Republic | Cent.Inst.Isotop. Radiat. | Onions (600 t/y) | 1983 |
| | Res. (Weideroda) | Garlic (4 t/y) | |
| | Queis Agric. Coop. (Spickendorf) | Onions (4,000 t/y) | 1986 |
| | VEB Prowiko (Shoenebeck) | Enzyme solution (300 t/y) | 1986 |
| Hungary | Agroster (Budapest) | Spices (200 t/y) | 1982 |
| | | Wine cork (100 m3) | |
| Israel | Sorvan Radiation Ltd. (Yavne) | Spices (120 t/y) | 1986 |
| Japan | Shihoro Agricultural Cooperative (Hokkaido) | Potatoes (20,000 t/y) | 1973 |
| Korea, Republic of | Korea Advance Energy Research Inst. (Seoul) | Garlic powder | 1985 |
| Netherlands | Gammaster (Ede) | Spices (100 t/y) | 1978 |
| | | Frozen products, poultry, spices, dehydrated vegetables, rice, dehydrated blood, egg powder, packaging materials | |

**Table 4 (cont'd)**

| Nation | Company (City) | Food Item (tons per year) | Starting Date |
|---|---|---|---|
| | Pilot Plant for Food Irradiation (Wageningen) | Spices | 1978 |
| Norway | Institute for Energy Technology (Kjeller) | Spices (500 t/y) | 1982 |
| South Africa | Nuclear Development Corp. | Fruits, meats, onions, potatoes | 1981 |
| | ISO-STER | Spices, dehydrated vegetables | |
| | High Energy Processing | Fruits | 1982 |
| USA | Radiation Technology, Inc. | Spices (500 t/y) | 1984 |
| | Isomedix, Inc. | Spices (500 t/y) | 1984 |
| | Radiation Sterilizer, Inc. | Spices (500 t/y) | |
| USSR | Odessa Port Elevator RDU (Odessa) | Grains (400,000 t/y) | 1983 |
| Yugoslavia | Ruder Boskovic Institute (Zagreb) | Black pepper | 1985 |

(Source: Food Irradiation Newsletter, Vol. 10, No. 2, November 1986, pp. 49-51.)

energy level is usually expressed in electron volts (eV). Above approximately 10 to 15 million electron volts (MeV), it is possible for significant amounts of radioactivity to be created. It is, therefore, important that only lower-energy ionizing radiations are used in irradiation of food.

Even so, it is still possible for some compounds in the food to be made radioactive. Below the 10-MeV level, however, the amount of this induced radioactivity is small, and it decays very rapidly. If foods are stored before use, the level of radiation is likely to be insignificant and well within the range of the natural radioactivity already found in food.[12]

The other way food may become contaminated with radioactivity is if the radioactive source is damaged. Obviously, great care should be taken to prevent this kind of accident.

Thus, provided irradiation is properly controlled, food should

### Table 5: Commercial Facilities Planned for Treating Food/Feed

| Member States | No. of Facilities | Location |
|---|---|---|
| Australia | 1 | Brisbane |
| Bangladesh | 2 | Dhaka, Chittagong |
| Canada | 1 | Quebec |
| China | 4 | Langzhou, Beijing, Zhen Shen, Zhenzhou |
| Cuba | 1 | Havana |
| France | 4 | Bretagne, Marseille, Orsay-Cedex, Orleans |
| Hungary | 1 | Budapest |
| Israel | 1 | Yavne |
| Italy | 1 | Fucino |
| Korea, Republic of | 2 | Seoul |
| Malaysia | 1 | Kuala Lumpur |
| New Zealand | 1 | Auckland |
| Pakistan | 1 | Lahore |
| Poland | 2 | Poznan, Przysucha |
| Thailand | 1 | Bangkok |
| US | 6 | Washington, Iowa, Alaska Oklahoma, Hawaii, Florida |
| Vietnam | 1 | Hanoi |
| Total | 31 | |

(Source: Food Irradiation Newsletter, Vol. 10, No. 2, November 1986, p. 52. Byproducts and Utilization Program, US DOE, 1986.)

not become measurably radioactive.

## Radioactive Sources for Food Irradiation

It has been suggested that the nuclear wastes from power stations be used as a radioactive source for food irradiation.[13] This is not immediately feasible because these wastes contain a wide range of radioactive materials, some emitting radiation with energy above the critical level.[12]

Two radioactive materials have been identified that are suitable and have energies considered low enough to be safe for use in food irradiation: cobalt 60 and cesium 137.

Cobalt 60 gives off two gamma rays of 1.17 and 1.33 MeV, and cesium 137 gives off 0.66 MeV gamma radiation. A mixture of cesium 137 and cesium 134 can also be used. Radiation from these radioactive isotopes is well below the 10-MeV threshold, and after storage there should be no measurable levels of induced radioactivity.

Disposal of radioactive cesium currently presents a considerable problem because of the quantities produced in nuclear wastes from reactors and the length of time they take to decay. The nuclear energy and weapons industries are therefore eager to find commercial uses for cesium. On the other hand, the viability of using this source depends on the continuing existence of the nuclear power program.[13]

Cesium in particular presents some storage problems because it is used in a water-soluble form and hence can cause greater environmental contamination in the event of any break in the tube in which it is sealed. Because its energy level is only about half that of cobalt, considerably more cesium is needed to give the same exposure to the food, and the ratio of maximum dose (on the outside) to minimum dose (in the middle of the food) is much greater.

The other possible sources of irradiation include beams of electrons, and x-rays created when a metal target is bombarded with electrons. These machine sources give off a wide spectrum of energies, and greater care must be taken to ensure that the maximum energy is below the 10-MeV threshold. Electrons do not penetrate materials as far as gamma or x-rays do, and so are only useful for irradiating the surface of foods.[12]

## Radiation Doses

*Dose* is commonly used to mean either of two distinct things: the amount of radiation received or, in the case of exposure to people, the amount of biological damage done. In measuring the dose to food we are concerned about the amount of energy that has been deposited as a result of irradiation. The old unit for dose was the rad; this is now being replaced by the gray (Gy). Very large doses up to 1 million rads are being considered for food irradiation. Therefore, the doses are more often given in megarads (Mrad) or kiloGrays (kGy), a million rad (1 Mrad) = 10 kGy (10,000 Gray).

To give some idea of the scale of these doses, the making of a chest x-ray film will deliver about 10 millirad (0.01 rad), and an average dose from natural background radiation will give about 100 millirad (0.1 rad) per year. The food irradiation dose is therefore 10 million to 100 million times these common doses.

The changes produced in the food increase as the dose goes up. This applies to both the desired and the undesirable changes.[12,14]

## Uses of Food Irradiation

As was just explained, radiation produces chemical changes in the food, and these in turn have biological effects. In some cases the exact mechanisms are still not fully understood. The following effects can be produced:

*Radurization:* low doses, usually below 100,000 rad (1 kGy)

- Sprouting of vegetables such as potatoes and onions can be inhibited so that they keep longer (5,000 to 15,000 rad: 0.05 to 0.15 kGy).
- Ripening of some fruits can be delayed so that they keep longer and can be transported longer distances (20,000 to 50,000 rad: 0.2 to 0.5 kGy).
- Insects in grains such as wheat and rice, or in spices and some fruits, can be rendered sterile. This may replace current methods involving gas storage or fumigation treatments for insect disinfestation that are hazardous to workers, and could reduce losses of foods.

*Radicidation:* medium doses, between 0.1 and 1.0 Mrad (1-10 kGy)

- Killing insects and other food parasites can involve higher doses than those that merely keep them from breeding in the food (30,000 to 600,000 rad: 0.3 to 6.0 kGy) and will not, of course, remove the dead parasites from the food.
- The number of microorganisms that lead to food spoiling, such as yeasts, molds, and bacteria can be reduced, and the life of foods can thereby be extended or the risk of food poisoning reduced. This may be important in the case of salmonella in chicken or fish.

*Radappertization:* high doses, above 1 Mrad (10 kGy)

- At extremely large doses, higher in fact than the 1 million rad (10 kGy) doses being proposed at present, food can be completely sterilized by the killing of all bacteria and viruses. This process might be used for meat products, allowing them to be kept indefinitely.[12]

These doses are only approximate. The actual dose depends on the thickness and density of the food package being irradiated as well as the desired effect. For bulk spices, doses of up to 3 million rads (30 kGy) can be used to kill insects and contaminating bacteria.[15]

These effects can be said to extend the shelf life of foods—the time it takes before stored food becomes unsaleable. In these cases, irradiation is used as a preservative.

## Improvement of Food by Irradiation

In addition to the food preservation benefits claimed for irradiation, a number of other "improvements" in quality have been claimed.[16] One is the improvement of baking and cooking quality of wheat, including the ability to add up to 15% soy flour to wheat flour without loss of baking quality. Irradiation also "improves" the elasticity and volume of dough in bread making. A number of additives are currently used to increase the bulk and the water and air content of the standard white loaf. Yeast can be stimulated by irradiation, leading to faster bread-making.[14] While this has obvious benefits to the large baking companies, it is a matter of opinion whether it leads to an improvement in bread quality.[17,18]

Irradiated barley can increase its yield during malting by 7%—a fact of interest to the brewing industry. Irradiation can be used to "age" spirits,[19] and irradiated grapes yield more juice when processed, possibly benefiting the fruit juice, wine-making, and distillery industries. Irradiated sugar solutions can be used as anti-oxidants, possibly replacing other chemicals used for this purpose in processed and prepared foods.

The time needed to reconstitute and cook dehydrated vegetables including peas and green beans, is reduced if they are irradiated. Since cooking times for dehydrated foods are already very short, it is debatable whether this provides any real benefit.

It is claimed that irradiation enhances the flavor of carrots, and the suggestion has been made that it could be used for tenderizing meat.[12]

It has been suggested that contaminated or spoiled food can be sterilized by irradiation and so made safe for human consumption. However, the joint expert committee of the WHO/FAO/IAEA has explicitly said that irradiation should not be used to make an unsuitable product saleable for human consumption and that food should always be wholesome before irradiation. There are, however, some who argue that this should be considered.[20] As we will show in Chapter 5, some cases of irradiation being used to conceal contamination have been documented.[21]

Most of the basic mechanisms of these "favorable" changes in food quality are not fully understood.[2,12,14] On balance, most of the uses just described are not necessities. They are either luxuries or techniques that may benefit the manufacturer but provide no clear benefit to the consumer.

Other non-food, but food-related, uses include modification of starches for the paper and textile industries, and radurization of gelatin for use in the photofilm industry.

Thus we find irradiation to be a potentially dangerous technology with its own needs for regulation and control, but one that is already in use on a small scale in several countries. It would appear to have some beneficial applications—certainly to food processors and possibly food retail sales outlets. If irradiation is properly controlled, food should not be made any more radioactive than it already is. If these were the only issues, there would seem to be little reason to be concerned beyond ensuring that the process is properly regulated and controlled. Unfortunately, as we shall see, there are other issues that give us grave cause for concern.

---

REFERENCES

1. John W. Gofman. *Radiation and Human Health*. San Francisco: Sierra Club Books, 1981.

2. P. S. Elias and A. J. Cohen. *Radiation Chemistry of Major Food Components*. Amsterdam and New York: Elsevier Biomedical Press, 1977.

3. See T. Webb and R. Collingwood. *Radiation and Health—A Graphic Guide*. London: Camden Press, 1987. *Radiation on the Job*. Tape Slide Presentation for Canadian Union of Public Employees. Radiation and Health Information Service, Ottawa, Canada, 1983. Also, C. Ryle, J. Garrion, T. Webb. *Radiation Your Health at Risk*. Radiation and Health Information Service, Cambridge, England, 1980.

4. R. Bertell. *No Immediate Danger—Prognosis for a Radioactive Earth*. London: The Women's Press, 1985.

5. J. G. Brennan, J. R. Butters, N. D. Cowell, A. E. V. Lilley. *Food Engineering Operations*. New York and Barking, UK: Elsevier-Applied Science Publications, 1976.

6. *Food Irradiation Processing*. Proceedings of a Symposium, Washington, DC, March 4-8, 1985. Jointly organized by the IAEA and FAO; IAEA, Vienna, 1985.

7. US Agency for International Development. Draft Feasibility Study. Washington, DC, May 1985.

8. Food Irradiation Response Newsletter. Santa Cruz, CA, December 1986/ January 1987.

9. Nuclear Regulatory Commission. Active NRC Licenses—Irradiators other >10,000 curies, September, 1986. NRC In-House Irradiation Facilities, September, 1986.

10. Terry Garrett. Isotron Profits Expected to Exceed £1 Million Mark. *Financial Times* (London), 1 July 1985.

11. South Manchester Health Authority. Appraisal of Catering Methods. Manchester, England, 1985.

12. Edward S. Josephson and Martin S. Peterson, eds. *Preservation of Food by Ionizing Radiation* (3 vols.). Florida: CRC Press, Vol. 1 1982, Vols. 2 & 3 1983.

13. R. S. Hannan. *Scientific and Technical Problems Involved in Using Ionizing Radiations for the Preservation of Food*. Dept. of Scientific and Industrial Research, Food Investigation Special Report No. 61, London: HMSO, 1955.

14. P. S. Elias and A. J. Cohen. *Recent Advances in Food Irradiation*. Amsterdam and New York: Elsevier Biomedical Press, 1983.

15. Department of Health and Human Services. Food and Drug Administration 21 CFR Part 179, Irradiation in the Production, Processing and Handling of Food; Final Rule. 51 Federal Register 13376 at 13385, Washington, DC, April 18, 1986.

16. *Improvement of Food Quality by Irradiation*. Proceedings of Panel, June 1973, Organized by FAO/IAEA Division of Atomic Energy in Food and Agriculture IAEA ST1/PUB/370, 1974.

17. *Our Daily Bread—Who Makes the Dough*. British Society for Social Responsibility in Science, Agricapital Group, London, 1978.

18. C. Walker and G. Cannon. *The Food Scandal*. London: Century Publishing, 1985.

19. P. S. Elias. Irradiation of Food. *Environmental Health*, October, 1982.

20. *Food Irradiation Now*. Symposium in Ede, The Netherlands, by Gammaster. 21 October 1981. Martinus Nijhof and Dr. W. Junk, 1982.

21. Irradiated Foods: Illegal Importation. Early Day Motion, House of Commons Order Paper, London, April 9, 1986.

# CHAPTER 3

# IS FOOD
# IRRADIATION SAFE?

THE JOINT EXPERT Committee of the International Atomic Energy Agency, the World Health Organization, and the Food and Agriculture Organization of the United Nations says that food irradiation is safe.[1] In Britain the Advisory Committee on Irradiated and Novel Foods says it is safe.[2] The European Economic Community's Scientific Committee for Food[3] and experts from the food and irradiation industries say it is safe.[4,5,6] Who are we to say it is not?

The answer to that question is to pose another. Are we being asked to take the word of experts, or is there conclusive evidence, backed up by scientific research that can be referred to and checked by independent researchers?

Some of those who have been lobbying for irradiation have suggested that 40 years of research show there are no safety problems whatsoever.[7] This is untrue. Ignoring or discounting evidence and studies that suggest damage from irradiated foods does not make this evidence go away. The first research done by the United States Army was used to obtain clearance for can-packed bacon in 1963, but clearance was subsequently withdrawn in 1968 when the Food and Drug Administration (FDA) found the research to be flawed. The FDA found that significant adverse effects were produced in animals fed irradiated food and that major deficiencies existed in the conduct of some experiments. The adverse effects included decreases in survival of weaned young for animals fed irradiated bacon and greater losses of young for those eating bacon exposed to higher doses of radiation.[8]

This same 40 years of research presumably also includes the subsequent research done in the United States when the work was turned over to Industrial Biotest Limited (IBT). Three officials of IBT were convicted in the federal courts in 1983 for doing fraudulent research for government and industry.[8] The government uncovered such problems as failure to conduct routine analyses, premature death of thousands of rodents from unsanitary laboratory conditions, faulty record-keeping, and suppression of unfavorable findings. Prior to the convictions, which were unrelated to food irradiation studies, the Army had declared the beef and pork feeding studies being conducted by IBT in default for similar contract violations. The Army discovered

> missing records, unallowable departures from testing protocol, poor quality work, and incomplete disclosure of information on the progress of the studies.[8]

The government lost about $4 million and 6 years' worth of animal feeding study data on food irradiation.[8] Some of this early discredited work is still used as part of the "scientific" basis for official assurances on food safety.

In this chapter we review some of the key issues: the possible hazards from chemical changes in the food, the adequacy of safety testing and the reviews undertaken by various governments, animal and human feeding trials, and microbiological hazards.

## Toxic Chemicals

Properly controlled, irradiation should not make food radioactive; the amount of induced radioactivity is extremely small and will die away very rapidly. It is certainly undetectable against the background levels of radiation in our food from natural sources and the fallout from nuclear weapons tests and accidents that have occurred since 1945. The first concern, therefore, is not radioactivity but the possibility of creating toxic chemicals in the food.

As noted earlier, bombarding any material with radiation can alter its chemical structure. The first stage of this process is the creation of "free radicals," highly reactive parts of the original chemical structures that have been split and that carry either positive or negative charges. A free radical rapidly combines with another radical of opposite charge. In some cases this can lead to recombination of the original molecule. In most cases it does not, and a completely new chemical can be created.

The chemicals created in the irradiated food are called "radiolytic products" or "radiolytes." Many of these are similar to those that occur in other forms of food processing, such as cooking. Some, however, are unique to irradiation.[9,10,11]

Because of the complexity of the reactions, it is difficult to identify all these radiolytic products and to test them in the usually accepted way by which, for example, chemical additives are tested. Initially, irradiated foods were fed to animals. Although the results have been reassuring overall, testing of a potential hazard usually involves feeding large quantities of the chemical. Testing by merely feeding the food is inadequate. Only small quantities of the unique radiolytes exist in the food. Testing can therefore miss underlying problems or long-term hazards.

More recently, a number of radiolytic products have been isolated and more normal high-dose testing has been done on them.[9] Again, the results have been claimed as reassuring. Even though some adverse effects have been found in experimental conditions, it is claimed that they are not likely to occur with irradiated foods under practical conditions, i.e., provided they conform to the international Codex Alimentarius standards and the guidelines developed by the Joint Expert Committee of the FAO/IAEA/WHO.[9]

It must be noted that the FAO/IAEA/WHO committee initially required testing on all irradiated food products. In 1976 this requirement was removed; results from one food could be applied to another, provided that the doses were below a limit of 1 million rad (10 kGy).[12] The Food and Drug Administration, however, insists that food irradiated in the medium-dose range could contain enough unique radiolytes to warrant toxicological study—hence the requirement that all foods irradiated above 100,000 rad (1 kGy) in the United States are required to be tested.

Clearly the dose is a critical factor. The higher the dose, the more radiolytic chemicals are created and the greater the potential risk. Initially, the FAO/IAEA/WHO specified both the maximum and minimum doses to be used in giving clearance to particular foods.[12] The minimum dose guaranteed that the food would have the changes expected of it, and the maximum guaranteed that undesired effects would be limited. In 1980, this requirement was changed and only an *average* dose was specified. In doing so, the committee accepted that doses up to 50% greater than this average could result.[1] In some quarters, this has been interpreted as giving clearance for maximum doses to be 1.5 million rad (15 kGy).[10] In the United States, the maximum dose is 100,000 rad. The use of cesium, with its low penetrating power, can result in wide differences between maximum and minimum doses unless the packages being irradiated are thin.

Thus, although testing has been undertaken over a number of years, and the dose ranges within which irradiated food can be regarded as safe have been defined, there has been a steady relaxing of the requirements for testing and for control of doses. In our opinion, these changes appear to have more to do with commercial considerations than public health.

The public needs far more information than simple statements that irradiated food is "safe." The public needs to know about the scientific uncertainty that underlies these statements from the expert bodies and to be given details of some of the adverse effects that have been found.

For chemicals that can cause cancer or genetic defects, it is safest to assume that there is no safe level of exposure to such chemicals; any dose can cause the initial damage that develops into a cancer. Damage to the genetic blueprint may cause miscarriage or defects in future generations. The fact that a chemical change is small does not eliminate the risk. When even a very small risk is spread over a large enough population, or a long enough time period, some damage is inevitable.[13]

## Evidence or Opinion?

There are problems involved in testing irradiated foods. Normal tests for chemical safety require isolation of the chemical and feeding it in large quantities to animals on the grounds that if no problems are found with high doses, then small doses should be safe. Isolating and testing all these chemical products would be a massive task. It may be that the normal animal testing program is inappropriate for irradiation. The fact remains that the 1976 decision of the FAO/IAEA/WHO expert committee to relax the requirements for testing of irradiated foods means that the chemical products of irradiation have not been tested with the same stringency required, say, of chemical additives. We have every reason to be concerned about many permitted food additives in use today.[14] Any less stringent testing program does not inspire confidence.

On the question of the assurances of food safety being based on fact or opinion, the fact is that neither the FAO/IAEA/WHO joint committee nor the British government Advisory Committee provide detailed references to the scientific literature to support their conclusions. Neither does the summary report of the opinion given by the Scientific Committee for Food to the European Commission in 1986.[3] This committee claims that it reviewed over 500 original studies from the Federal Research Center for Nutrition in Karlsruhe, West Germany, where most of the recent work done for the IAEA on food irradiation has been undertaken. It is to be hoped that the full report, now promised for 1987, will remedy this deficiency in a basic principle of scientific reporting: that sources for the evidence are cited so that they can be checked by independent critics.

Presumably, one who is an expert in the field, and knows of all the research being done, may be able to infer which evidence is being used to support which claim. One who is not has no chance of untangling the mystique, but will have to trust (or doubt) the experts. We happen to believe that democratic decision-making deserves better than this. Given the current public mood on many similar issues, the reaction to the suggestion that we should "trust the experts" is more likely to be doubt than trust,[15] and this will damage the chances that irradiation will be introduced even in those areas where, on balance, the benefits may outweigh the risks.

There is, in fact, a body of scientific literature indicating adverse effects from feeding irradiated foods. It may be that we can safely ignore this evidence on the basis of flaws in the data or on the basis of systematic investigation of all the possible effects and potential causes. If so, we respectfully ask to see this evidence. So far it has not been forthcoming. We simply cannot understand how the various committees could have undertaken to review the available scientific evidence without some systematic plan, which involves looking at each area of concern, identifying the studies indicating that there is or may be a problem, similarly identifying those that did not find the problem, and weighing all the various strengths and weaknesses of both sets of studies against objective criteria. This would have been required of an undergraduate university degree student, let alone some of the world's leading experts advising governments and the United Nations on an issue of such importance.

The best that can be said of many of these reviews is that they offer the opinion that there are no "special" safety problems associated with consumption of irradiated food if it is properly controlled, but that they fail to back up these opinions with facts. They are also, as we will see, noticeably silent on the systems for control of the technology and how to prevent its abuse. We can hardly be blamed for not finding these opinions reassuring.

The situation in the United States is marginally better than in the rest of the world. Irradiation is governed by the 1958 Food, Drug and Cosmetics Act,[16] which classifies irradiation as an "additive" and requires users of irradiation to petition the FDA for clearances on specific foods and show, by supporting evidence, that the food will be safe. So far the FDA has given clearances for food only up to 100,000 rad (1 kGy)—one tenth of the internationally recommended limit. The exception is that in the United States, spices can receive up to 3 million rad—three times the international level.

In practice, however, it is possible that foods will get higher doses than those permitted. In a petition to the FDA to allow higher irradiation doses for spices, R. L. Hall, Vice President of McCormick & Company, Inc., stated, "In existing large-scale irradiators, it is quite likely that an overdose of up to 250% can be expected."[17] It is unclear at this time whether the FDA's limits are maximum doses or whether, like the recommended Codex standard, they are to be interpreted as average doses.

## How Adequate Are the FDA's Review Processes?

A recent review of the process adopted in granting approval for irradiation of pork shows that the FDA did make some attempt to evaluate the strengths and weaknesses of the studies both for and against the existence of harmful effects. Some objective criteria were drawn up by which studies were to be judged acceptable. Using these criteria, the FDA discarded all the evidence suggesting that there were adverse effects. FDA staff also found that they had to discard most of the studies indicating that irradiation was safe by the same criteria. The result was that they were left with only five studies on which to base the approval for irradiation of pork.

Dr. George Pauli of the FDA's Food Safety Division admitted that neither the FDA nor any other review body has so far attempted to show that the safety concerns raised by many of the studies can be discounted by reference to other studies that did not find these problems under similar conditions.[10] Such a review might, on balance, show that the risks could be considered slight and perhaps acceptable. It would also show the extent of scientific uncertainty that exists. More important, it would indicate the areas where further research is needed and provide both legislators and consumers with the basis for deciding whether they wish to accept the outstanding risks in return for the benefits of irradiation.

In fact, the FDA's 1986 clearances are not even based on the few studies it approves of. Rather, they are based on a theoretical estimate of the number and amount of unique radiolytic chemicals likely to be created. In 1980, the FDA concluded that the levels of new chemicals are so low that doses up to 100,000 rads (1 kGy) are acceptable.[19] This appears to some critics to be a reinterpretation of the law that requires proof of the safety of irradiation by animal testing studies.[20] It may even be illegal.

## Evidence of Cause for Concern

The problems of investigating the safety of irradiated foods are compounded by the lack of credibility of some of the research done by the United States Army and IBT. Lethal effects from feeding irradiated food to mice have been observed. Other studies have not confirmed these effects.[9] Some animals fed irradiated food have been found to have reduced growth rates, lower birth weights for offspring, changes in white blood cells, and kidney damage. The chemical agents responsible have not been identified, but some of the changes may be due to effects on the body's immune system. There is also a suggestion that vitamin reduction in irradiated foods is a cause of some of these health effects.[10] Studies have found increased incidence of tumors, which suggests that cancers may be caused by long-term consumption of irradiated foods.[3,21] Other studies have not detected significant increases in tumors. A similar conflict of evidence exists over whether irradiated food can cause genetic mutations. The balance is in favor of the view that they do not, but some uncertainty remains.[10]

With cancer and genetic damage, we are concerned that even very small quantities of a harmful chemical may cause the damage. Dr. George Tritsch, a researcher at the Roswell Park Memorial Institute Cancer Research Center in Buffalo, New York, has expressed concern about exposure of people to possible carcinogens like those which may be created in small amounts in irradiated foods. He notes that "...a single carcinogenic insult is all that is needed to produce a malignant neoplasm a decade or more later."[22]

As early as 1979, a review of food irradiation literature by J. Barna for the Hungarian Academy of Sciences identified hundreds of adverse effects in animals relating to the feeding of irradiated food.[23] Study results were classified as either neutral, adverse, or beneficial. Each study could have several outcomes, since studies could address more than one issue. Barna found 1,414 adverse effects, 185 beneficial effects, and 7,191 neutral effects. For bacon, he found 86 neutral study results, 31 adverse study results, and no beneficial results. For soybeans, he found 60 adverse study results, no beneficial results, and 26 neutral study results. For sucrose, he found 39 adverse study results, 38 neutral, and one beneficial. For corn oil, he found 13 adverse, five neutral, and no beneficial results.

The results of extensive animal feeding studies conducted by Raltech Scientific Service for the federal government were reported in 1984. Some results suggested safety, but according to the Department of Agriculture reviewer, Donald W. Thayer, chief of the Food Safety Laboratory at the Agricultural Research Service,

> Two of the studies...had some possible adverse findings which will require careful consideration before the process can be declared safe.[21]

The nutritional and toxicological studies evaluated five diets: (a) commercial laboratory diet (no chicken control), (b) frozen chicken (control), (c) thermally processed chicken, (d) cobalt 60 processed chicken, and (e) electron irradiated chicken. Although Dr. Thayer did not highlight the problem, one study to explore the effects on offspring had to be terminated prematurely because of excessive mortality among offspring in all diet groups. The study, intended to last two years, was cancelled after only nine months. Instead of repeating the study to determine the true long-term reproductive effects, the researchers declared the process safe on their limited nine-month data.[24]

In studies of mice fed test diets from birth to death, survival of both sexes was significantly reduced for those fed gamma-irradiated food, and the group eating gamma-irradiated chicken had the highest incidence of several tumors among those analyzed. To counter claims of possible harm, the National Toxicology Program assembled a new panel to review the slides on lesions in the test animals, and this panel declared that the lesions were not cancerous. Nonetheless, this panel failed to explain the increased number of deaths among the animals eating gamma-irradiated chicken. It did demonstrate disagreement among experts.

In another portion of the Raltech study, fruit flies (*Drosophila*), which are commonly used to test for mutations, were fed test diets. For this portion of the study, a sixth group was fed a known hazardous chemical (TRIS) as a positive control. The TRIS was expected to show dominant lethal mutations. Table 6 shows the results of the study.

Dr. Thayer reported
> ...an unexplained significant reduction in the production of off-spring in cultures of *D. melanogaster* reared on gamma-irradiated chicken. This response was dose related and was not overcome by the addition of vitamin supplements.[21]

### Table 6: Number of Drosophila Offspring

| Compound | Average Number of Offspring |
|---|---|
| Negative control (no chicken meat) | 720.6 |
| Frozen control chicken | 332.7 |
| Thermally processed chicken | 404.4 |
| TRIS (@ 100 ppm) positive control (no chicken meat) | 269.9 |
| Electron-irradiated chicken | 160.0 |
| Gamma-irradiated chicken | 57.1 |

(Source: Raltech Scientific Services, Inc. The Final Report. Evaluation of the Mutagenicity of Irradiated Sterilized Chicken by the Sex-Linked Recessive Test in *Drosophila Melanogaster*. Contract DAMD 17-76-C-6047, June 15, 1979.)

In fact, the table reprinted here (which was not part of the Thayer report) demonstrates that the fruit flies fed gamma-irradiated chicken had seven times fewer offspring than those fed thermally processed (cooked) chicken. A dose-response pattern occurred, with higher concentrations of gamma-irradiation of chicken producing fewer offspring.

Food irradiation proponents declared the results irrelevant, since fruit flies don't normally eat chicken. Table 6 clearly shows that fruit flies consuming no chicken had far more offspring, but, particularly in view of the study results, it is certainly appropriate to compare the groups eating the chicken diets. The positive control, the chicken diet with a known hazardous chemical, led to better reproduction than either the electron- or gamma-irradiated diets. While the fruit flies eating electron-irradiated chicken had about three times more offspring than those fed gamma-treated chicken, they still had less than half the offspring of the flies fed unirradiated, frozen chicken.

Despite these findings, in an article published in Cereal Foods World in 1984 Dr. Thayer concluded:

> On balance, the studies on radappertized chicken conducted by the US army and various contractors strongly supports the process' safety, but these are some potentially serious adverse results, which must be considered when the FDA examines these studies.[25]

Many of these studies involved much higher doses than those proposed for commercial irradiation. The quantities of a particular radiolytic chemical may increase with the dose. However, the type of radiolytic chemical change is likely to be the same whatever the dose. We are concerned that even small quantities of some chemicals could be hazardous.[23]

Indeed, the European Committee for Food states, of the study feeding chicken to mice,

> the use of a higher dose would amplify any effects of irradiation and [this study] might be a sensitive indication of a carcinogenic effect which could also be present at lower doses.[3]

## Human Studies

There have also been some studies on feeding irradiated foods to people.

Conscientious objectors were fed irradiated foods in a university study in 1953. The men were given physical examinations before and after a two-week diet of irradiated foods, and no immediate damage was observed. Unfortunately, no long-term follow-up was built into this research.[26]

The United States Army has performed trials in which people consumed several irradiated foods. There is little information in the scientific literature on these studies. Chinese researchers reported that in 1982 they were "unable to get the information in detail."[27]

The Chinese have done most of the work on feeding irradiated foods to human volunteers. Reports on these have been reassuring. Studies on feeding potatoes,[28] rice,[29] mushrooms,[30] meat products,[31] and peanuts[32] all found no adverse effects.

These studies were followed by eight human volunteer studies in 1982. The foods investigated included rice, mushrooms, sausage, peanuts, meat products, and potatoes. There were also two studies in which 60 to 66% of the whole diet was irradiated. These extended over 7 to 15 weeks and took into consideration a variety of health factors. In no case was any difference found between the volunteers in the experimental group and those in the control group, who were on a normal unirradiated diet.

A subsequent human volunteer study[27] in 1984 tested the effects of irradiating the whole diet, consisting of 35 different foods. This involved 70 volunteers and lasted for 90 days. The only possible adverse effect noted was a small increase in polyploidy, a defect in the chromosomes of blood cells. This was not thought to be significant, as a similar increase in polyploidy was also found in the control group.

Polyploidy was also observed in a study on feeding freshly irradiated wheat to malnourished children, conducted by the National Institute of Nutrition (NIN) at the Council of Medical Research, Hyderabad, in India. Children fed freshly irradiated wheat developed polyploidy, whereas children in a control group, fed a similar but unirradiated diet, did not show this problem. Once the children were taken off the irradiated wheat diet, their blood patterns gradually returned to normal. The research indicated that if the wheat were stored for a period of time (several months), the blood abnormalities probably would not occur.[33]

The treatment of this issue by both the FDA and the British ACINF highlights the concern we expressed earlier over the way that scientific evidence is handled and possible concerns dismissed.

It was suggested in November 1984, at the American Nuclear Society/European Nuclear Society joint meeting held in Washington, D.C., that the study was fraudulent.[34] A panel member even claimed that the study was repudiated by the Director of the Institute conducting the study.[35] We wrote to the Institute, and the Director responded that they stand behind their study. In fact, similar problems with freshly irradiated wheat have been demonstrated in the blood of both monkeys and rodents.[36]

In its final ruling, the FDA stated:

> A committee of Indian scientists critically examined the techniques, the appropriateness of experimental design, the data collected, and the interpretations of NIN scientists who claimed that ingestion of irradiated wheat caused polyploidy in rats, mice, and malnourished children.[37]

The FDA goes on to say that the committee report was "presented to the Joint Expert Committee in 1976," (of the IAEA/FAO/WHO), although agency personnel later had to retract this claim.[38] The so-called committee of Indian scientists turned out to be two researchers who submitted a confidential report to the Ministry of Health and Family Planning in India. The report was requested by the ministry because research undertaken by the Bhabba Atomic Research Centre (BARC) obtained different results from those found by NIN. BARC was seeking approval to irradiate food. NIN responded to the two-person "committee" with a report to the Indian government verifying the validity of their work and refuting in detail the claims and conclusions of the critical report. They also included independent evaluations of their data by two of the country's foremost cytogeneticists.[39]

The ACINF report, referring to what can only be the Indian study, concluded that

> It was found that the abnormal cells disappeared within a few weeks after withdrawal of irradiated wheat from the diet, and we do not think that this transient phenomenon would have any harmful long term consequences.[2]

While this may be true for the Indian children involved in the study, it hardly reassures us that long-term consumption of irradiated food will be safe. Neither did it reassure the British Medical Association, whose Board of Science produced a report in March 1987 emphasizing that further research is needed in this area.[40]

## A Cancer Connection?

Polyploidy may be a significant health issue. Normally, we all have 46 chromosomes, which contain the blueprint for the cells' functions. Damage to the chromosomes can cause the cell to malfunction. With polyploidy there are extra complete sets of chromosomes, i.e., human polyploid cells may have two sets (92 chromosomes) or three sets (138 chromosomes), and so on. Polyploidy is rare in human cells. It can result from a simple failure to separate at cell division and is frequently seen in tumor cells, although this is only one example of the bizarre cell forms present in established tumors. Polyploid lymphocytes have been found in increasing numbers with age,[41] but, as yet, there is no evidence of a direct correlation with cancer incidence.[42] However, to quote the Indian study,[33]

> The long term health hazard significance of polyploidy seen in the children studied here who had received freshly irradiated wheat, is not clear. On this will depend the answer to the question whether irradiated wheat is safe for human consumption.

In the light of these observations, it is clear that a cautious approach must be adopted to the whole question of the mutagenic potential of irradiated wheat.

Scientists do not fully understand what mechanisms come into play in the formation of cancer, but it is widely believed that there is damage at the cell level, in particular to the chromosomes, that initiates the process, and that exposure to a secondary agent may be needed to promote the cancer.[43]

What is particularly worrying is that the initial effect of irradiation is to create free radicals, i.e., highly reactive chemical components created by splitting the more stable complex chemical structures in food. Free radicals are believed to be common cancer "promoters."[43,44] That is, they promote the second-stage developments that turn the initially damaged cells into malignant (i.e., cancerous) ones. Most of the free radicals created by irradiation rapidly recombine into stable chemical forms. However, some remain. One of the tests being developed to detect irradiated foods relies on detection of very small quantities of free radicals remaining in some foods for some time after irradiation.

Whatever the mechanisms involved in the chain of events from cell damage to cancer and/or genetic damage, few in the medical profession would regard an increase in polyploid cells as a trivial matter. The discovery of such changes in the blood of animals and humans fed irradiated diets is clearly cause for concern, though not in itself proof that eating irradiated foods causes such effects. It does require careful evaluation of all the scientific evidence.

There are other studies whose conclusions offer some reassurance, in that they did not find an increase in polyploidy. A closer look at the primary research reports, however, raises more doubts than are laid to rest. One of the reports refers to an eight-week feeding trial done in Cambridgeshire, England.[45] A group of rats fed an irradiated wheat-based diet was compared with a control group fed an un-irradiated diet. Unfortunately, this study did not address the issue of damage from freshly irradiated food. The wheat used had been irradiated two weeks before the start of the study and was thus ten weeks old at the end. In addition, the experimenters (to their credit) reported that on the eighth week they could not find the feed for the experimental animals and concluded that they must have fed it to the control group. After various changes were made in the study protocol to compensate for this, they could not find significant differences between the two groups. The results from the two experimenters who counted the numbers of polyploid cells showed no consistency, even though they were both investigating cells from the same animals. This indicates some of the problems of counting polyploid cells. By the same token, it weakens the strength of the initial Indian findings.

## Other Long-term Effects

Perhaps more worrying than any specific disease attributable to irradiated foods is the report of a 15-week study on rats fed a diet containing 70% freshly irradiated wheat (irradiated at 75,000 rad, or 0.75 kGy). These animals were found to have a lowered immune response, which suggests that irradiated food may inhibit resistance to fight off infections and lower the body's resistance to a wide range of diseases.[3]

The key issue appears to be whether there is a problem with freshly irradiated foods. It is entirely reasonable to expect that there will be a higher incidence of reactive chemicals in the food immediately after irradiation. With time, many of them will recombine to more stable forms, and some volatile chemicals may escape from the food. After a while the irradiated food becomes, chemically speaking, harder to distinguish from the unirradiated product. Any possible undesirable biological effects on human health will likely be considerably reduced.

If there is a problem with freshly irradiated produce, this will not, of itself, invalidate the use of irradiation. What will be needed, however, is a system that guarantees that the produce is stored for a suitable period before being consumed. A simple "do not sell before" or "do not consume before" date marking label put on the food at the time of irradiation may be all that is required.

In summary, we clearly need further research and a more open discussion of the available evidence on possible adverse effects of food irradiation. Failure in some instances to conduct appropriate experiments, attempts to deliberately misrepresent the work of third world scientists who have had reason to be concerned, and the offering of vague opinions from some national and international committees concerned with food irradiation do not help. The conclusions offered by such committees seem more designed to provide reassurance than scientific facts. They only add to the level of suspicion over the way that scientific testing of the safety of irradiated foods has been conducted.

## Microbiological Hazards

The effects of irradiation are not limited to chemical changes in the food. Irradiation is also used to kill the yeasts, molds, and bacteria that cause food to spoil. It will also render sterile any insects that infest it.

There is a possibility that irradiation causes mutations in viruses, insects, and bacteria in food, leading to more resistant strains.[13] There are numerous examples of insects developing resistance to pesticides. Could they become resistant or genetically altered by radiation?

Fortunately, most genetic changes are nonviable; i.e., insects or their offspring are most likely to be killed or rendered sterile. Some strains of resistant salmonellae have been developed by repeated irradiation under laboratory conditions. Radiation-resistant bacteria have been found in environments with high natural or artificial radiation levels,[10] and development of such resistance may be a problem around large irradiation plants.[9] Indeed, the ACINF stated

> Sub-lethal doses of ionizing radiation can produce chemical changes in genetic material of micro-organisms (mutations) leading to altered characteristics which will be propagated in subsequent generations. Such mutant micro-organisms could be more pathogenic than native forms. Also they might exhibit altered growth characteristics which would make them difficult to detect or identify, and thus interfere with the standard microbiological evaluation of irradiation. Mutants might also be more radiation resistant, and if they were to spread into the environment, they might contaminate food prior to irradiation and so render the process ineffective.[2]

Of greater concern, however, is the fact that, though irradiation can kill bacteria in food, it will not remove the toxins (chemical poisons) that have been created by the bacteria at the earlier stages of contamination. This is important, as we will see when we consider some of the abuses of irradiation in Chapter 5. It is the toxins created by bacterial contamination that are the real public health hazard.

Not all the microorganisms in food are harmful. Some perform useful functions, particularly in warning us that food is going bad by giving off a putrid smell. Yeasts and molds also compete with harmful bacteria and so provide natural controls on their growth. If this natural balance is destroyed, it is possible that the few remaining harmful bacteria can multiply rapidly without inhibition, and within a short time the problem can be greater than before irradiation.

Increased production of aflatoxins following irradiation was first found in 1973[46,49] and confirmed in 1976 and 1978 (Table 7). Aflatoxins are powerful agents for causing liver cancer. Their production was found to be stimulated by irradiation at doses approved by the FAO/IAEA/WHO expert committee.

## Table 7: Stimulation of Aflatoxin Production After Irradiation

| Food | Increase |
| --- | --- |
| wheat | increases with dose |
| corn | 31% |
| sorgum | 81% |
| millet | 66% |
| potatoes | 74% |
| onions | 84% |

(Source: Reference 49.)

Aflatoxins occur in damp environments on fungus spores on grains or vegetables. Control of humidity in storage becomes even more important in the case of irradiated than of nonirradiated foods.

One food in which this issue can be of concern is peanuts. Currently, some importers go to great lengths to ensure that imported nuts are not contaminated with aflatoxin-creating bacteria. They fear that if irradiation is legalized, suppliers may irradiate nuts to keep the bacterial count below the control levels. In doing so, the competing bacteria will also be destroyed, and within a short time after the importers have purchased what they believe to be "clean" peanuts, aflatoxin production could rapidly increase. It is the processors, not the foreign suppliers, who will be blamed by the consumer for any subsequent health hazard.

Other, more complicated and expensive tests can be used to detect aflatoxins. For some other toxins there are not, as yet, corresponding tests that can detect the chemical poisons in the absence of the bacteria that create them.

Another example of the possible effect of irradiation arises in the irradiation of chicken to reduce the risk of *Salmonella* food poisoning from chicken and fish. Irradiation of chicken could kill most of the *Salmonella* bacteria on chicken flesh, and also kill most of the yeasts and molds that are the natural competitors of *clostridium botulinum*— the bacterium that causes the much more serious food poisoning, botulism. It will also kill most of the organisms that cause the putrid odor when meat has gone bad. Yet, at the doses proposed, *c. botulinum* will not be killed. Under the right conditions (e.g., warmth and absence of air) the organisms could multiply and become a health hazard without the consumer's having detected any warning odor.[2,9,13,47]

With fish this is less likely. Lower doses will be used, and there should be enough spoilage organisms left to multiply along with the *c. botulinum* so that the food smells unacceptable when the botulism becomes a hazard.[9]

Clearly, such possibilities reinforce the need for strict control of both the irradiation process and the conditions under which irradiated food is packaged, stored, and handled. They may also severely limit the uses of irradiation. The USDA has set up a strict testing protocol for studies that will be needed before it will allow vacuum packaging of irradiated meat products.[48] It is clear from our conversations with USDA staff that botulism formation is the main concern. If irradiated foods cannot be packaged so as to prevent airborne recontamination by bacteria, then there is no way that the technology can fulfill many of the promises claimed for it. The food cannot be guaranteed to remain free from food poisoning organisms. Use of chemical preservatives, refrigeration, and even more rigorous hygiene practices in food handling will be needed, as well as irradiation.

## Summary of Our Concern

We are not saying that irradiated food is definitely unsafe or harmful. However, the testing program to date does indicate that some possibly harmful effects could occur and that they need proper investigation. The way these concerns have so far been dismissed is profoundly disturbing. They are frequently called "insignificant" or "not likely to occur in practice." The studies that find problems are discounted.

The expert bodies appear to change the rules by which we judge the validity of a test. To present an independent challenge to this process is like playing football while the referee is moving the goal posts. First the chemical products created by irradiation are to be tested like chemical additives, then they are not. It is to be sufficient to show that there are no harmful effects when the food itself is fed to animals. Then when this study shows unwanted results, the criteria for accepting the results from an animal feeding study are tightened up. Finally, when so few studies are left—either showing or failing to show harmful effects—that it looks as though we should go back and redo the whole testing program and get it right this time, the FDA removes the goal posts completely. Approval can now be based on estimates of the quantities of chemical products formed by irradiation, and the opinion they are so small as to present no hazard.

The public has a right to unbiased, objective information on the possible harmful effects of irradiation, and not bland reassurances that hide uncomfortable evidence under value judgments. It is the job of the democratic processes to decide whether the effects are significant and the risks acceptable, and to lay down the conditions under which any risks can be minimized. When science, scientific experts, and regulatory agencies enter this area to pre-empt discussion of these issues, we have reason to be concerned.

---

REFERENCES

1. World Health Organization. *Wholesomeness of Irradiated Food.* Report of Joint FAO/IAEA/WHO Expert Committee. WHO Technical Report Series No. 659, Geneva, 1981.

2. UK Government's Advisory Committee on Irradiated and Novel Foods. *Report on the Safety and Wholesomeness of Irradiated Foods.* London: HMSO, 1986.

3. Opinion of the Scientific Committee for Food Given to the European Commission. Brussels, 13 March 1986.

4. Robert Millar. *Coming Soon . . . Atom Rays That Keep Food Fresh. Daily Express* (London), 4 February 1985.

5. A. W. Holmes. Letter to Editor. *Observer* (London), 9 May 1985.

6. Frank Ley. In: Irradiation of Food Becoming Accepted, by John Young. *The Times* (London), 31 January 1983.

7. Atomic Industrial Forum, Inc. Background Information: An Introduction to Food Irradiation, September 1986.

8. US Government Accounting Office. *The Department of the Army's Food Irradiation Program—Is It Worth Continuing?* PSAD-78-146. Washington, DC, September 29, 1978.

9. Edward S. Josephson and Martin S. Peterson, eds. *Preservation of Food by Ionizing Radiation* (3 vols.). Florida: CRC Press, Vol. 1 1982, Vols. 2 & 3 1983.

10. P. S. Elias and A. J. Cohen. *Recent Advances in Food Irradiation.* Amsterdam and New York: Elsevier Biomedical Press, 1983.

11. P. S. Elias and A. J. Cohen. *Radiation Chemistry of Major Food Components.* Amsterdam and New York: Elsevier Biomedical Press, 1977.

12. World Health Organization. *Wholesomeness of Irradiated Food.* Report of Joint FAO/IAEA/WHO Expert Committee. WHO Technical Report Series No. 604, Geneva, 1977.

13. R. S. Hannan. *Scientific and Technical Problems Involved in Using Ionizing Radiations for the Preservation of Food.* Dept. of Scientific and Industrial Research, Food Investigation Special Report No. 61, London: HMSO, 1955.

14. Melanie Miller. *Danger! Additives at Work.* London Food Commission, 1985; and Melanie Miller. *Additives Information Pack.* London Food Commission, 1987.

15. *Food Irradiation.* Omnibus Research by Marplan Ltd. Conducted for the London Food Commission, London, January 1987.

16. Federal Food, Drug, and Cosmetic Act 21 USC Section 301 et. seq., 1986.

17. R. L. Hall, Vice President—Science and Technology, McCormick & Co., Inc. Citizen Petition to FDA, November 1, 1983, p. 2.

18. Conversation between Tony Webb and Dr. George Pauli, December 1986.

19. Bureau of Foods Recommendations for Evaluating the Safety of Irradiated Foods. Final Report. July 1980.

20. Kathleen M. Tucker, HEI, and Robert Alvarez, EPI. In re: Food Irradiation. Petition to FDA Docket No. 81N-0004, May 19, 1986.

21. D. W. Thayer. *Summary of Supporting Documents for Wholesomeness Studies of Pre-cooked (Enzyme Inactivated) Chicken Products in Vacuum Sealed Containers Exposed to Doses of Ionizing Radiation Sufficient to Achieve "Commercial Sterility."* US Department of Agriculture, Philadelphia, March 19, 1984.

22. George Tritsch. Letters to the Editor. *Chemical Engineering News,* July 21, 1986.

23. J. Barna. Compilation of Bioassay Data on the Wholesomeness of Irradiated Food Items. Vol. 8, *Acta Alimentaria* 3, 205, 1979.

24. Ralston Purina Co. Irradiation Sterilized Chicken: A Feeding Study in Rats. Contract No. 53-3K06-1-29, 69, July 1982.

25. Donald W. Thayer. Cereal Foods World, Vol. 29, No. 6, 356, 1984.

26. Kitty Tucker and Mark Rabinowitz. *More False Promises from the Nuclear Industry.* Health and Energy Institute, Washington, DC, December 1985.

27. Dai Yin. An Introduction of Safety Evaluation on Irradiated Foods in China. Paper to FAO/IAEA Seminar for Asia and the Pacific on the Practical Application of Food Irradiation, Shanghai, China, April 7-11, 1986.

28. Li Hao, et al. Feeding Trial of $\propto$-ray Irradiated Potato in Human Volunteers. *Proceedings of Food Hygiene Research,* 2(2):32-37, 1984.

29. Hou Yn Hua, et al. Feeding Trial of $\propto$-ray Irradiated Rice in Human Volunteers. *Proceedings of Food Hygiene Research,* 2(2):18-24, 1984.

30. He Zhiqian, et al. Study on Safety of Irradiated Mushroom to Human Body. *Proceedings of Food Hygiene Research,* 2(2):43-49, 1984.

31. Zhang Yan, et al. Feeding Trial of $\propto$-ray Irradiated Meat Products in Human Volunteers. *Proceedings of Food Hygiene Research,* 2(2):69-74, 1984.

32. Li Juesen, et al. Feeding Trial of $\propto$-ray Irradiated Peanut in Human Volunteers. *Proceedings of Food Hygiene Research,* 2(2):56-61, 1984.

33. C. Bhaskaram and G. Sadasivan. Effects of Feeding Irradiated Wheat to Malnourished Children. Vol. 28, *American Journal of Clinical Nutrition,* February 1975, pp. 130-135.

34. Alternative Uses for Nuclear Energy: Focus on Food Irradiation. ANS/ENS International Conference, Washington, DC, November 13, 1984.

35. Martin Welt. Radiation Technology, Inc. Memo. Subject: Food Irradiation Panel Update, November 14, 1984, p. 1.

36. Vijayalaxmi and G. Sadasivan. *International Journal of Radiation Biology,* 27 (2), 1975, p. 135, 283; Vijayalaxmi. Cytogenetic Studies in Monkeys Fed Irradiated Wheat *Toxicology,* Vol. 9, 1978, p. 181.

37. 51 Fed. Reg. 13376 at 13385, April 18, 1986.

38. FDA Erred Citing FAO/WHO Review of Indian Irradiated Wheat Study. Vol. 28, *Food Chemical News,* November 17, 1986, p. 17.

39. Chronology of Events Pertaining to the Indian Study. Compiled by Joel Hill from relevant correspondence for NCSFI, San Francisco, August 1986.

40. Irradiation of Foodstuffs. British Medical Association Board of Science, London: March 1987.

41. John Gofman. *Radiation and Human Health.* New York: Pantheon Books, 1983, chapter 3 (thorough treatment of chromosome damage by radiation).

42. Jacobs et al. *Nature,* 193, 591, 1962.

43. E. Boyland. Tumour Initiators, Promoters and Complete Carcinogens. *British Journal of Industrial Medicine,* 47, 716-718, 1984.

44. W. A. Pryor. *Free Radicals in Biology.* New York: Academic Press, 1977.

45. Tesh, Davidson, Walker, Palmer, Cozens, and Richardson. *Studies in Rats Fed a Diet Incorporating Irradiated Wheat.* International Project in the field of Food Irradiation, Karlsruhe. IFIP-R45.

46. Bullerman, et al. Use of Gamma Irradiation to Prevent Aflatoxin Production in Bread. Vol. 38, *Journal of Food Science,* 1238, 1973.

47. *Factors Influencing the Economical Application of Food Irradiation.* Proceedings of a Panel held in Venice, June 1971. Organized by FAO/IAEA Division of Atomic Energy on Food and Agriculture. IAEA ST1/PUB/331. Vienna, 1973. See also *Requirements for the Irradiation of Food on a Commercial Scale.* FAO/IAEA Division of Atomic Energy in Food and Agriculture. Vienna, 1974.

48. *Scheme and Critical Variables for a Limited Study on the Effects of Vacuum Packaging and Irradiation on the Outgrowth and Toxin Production of* Clostridium Botulinum *in Pork Loins.* US Department of Agriculture. Food Safety and Inspection Service, Washington, DC, June 1986.

49. E. Pryadorshini and P. B. Tuple. Effects of Graded Doses of Gamma Irradiation on Aflatoxin Production by Aspergillus Parasiticus in Wheat. *Cosmet Toxicology* No. 505, 1979. Aflatoxin Production on Irradiated Foods. *Cosmet Toxicology* No. 293, 1976.

# CHAPTER 4

# WHOLESOMENESS OF IRRADIATED FOOD?

IN THE ENGLISH language, "wholesomeness" is a word that combines the ideas of safe, nourishing, and health-promoting. Unfortunately, there is no similar word in other languages, which means that in the international debate about food irradiation, the word has been debased so that it only covers the absence of any harmful effects. As long as there are no harmful toxic chemicals, or the microbiological and nutritional changes in the food do not cause obvious problems, the various scientists feel able to declare irradiated food "wholesome."

This narrow approach ignores questions concerning damage to essential constituents of food, such as vitamins and polyunsaturated fatty acids. It also ignores the effect that the technology may have on dietary health, particularly for people whose diet is already deficient. It also dismisses the impact of the technology on the natural balance of microorganisms that make up the ecology of our food.

It may be possible to show that irradiation, properly controlled, does not produce particular harmful agents, or that the risk of such events is slight and likely to be acceptable. Even so, the term "wholesome" cannot be applied to foods that may still appear fresh but that have been significantly denatured, either by the process of irradiation or by the extended storage times that irradiation makes possible. There is a big difference between "safe for human consumption" and "wholesome." This is a distinction the public can and does make, and which they need to be able to continue to make as a fundamental right. Wholesomeness, and the thorny question of the labeling of irradiated foods so that the consumer is made aware of the changed nature of the food, are issues that cannot be separated.

The issue goes deeper than protecting the individual's right to know what is being done to food. We also need to consider the effects on public health of changes in the general diet that result when a significant portion of the diet comes from irradiated foods.

Public health agencies and nutritionists are beginning to get across the message that we need significant changes in the North American diet if we are to tackle some of the major causes of ill health, not least the heavy toll of coronary heart disease.[1] The same is true for most of Europe.[2] It is widely recognized that we need to cut down on the amount of fat and, within the remaining fat content of the diet, to substitute unsaturated fats for some of the saturated fats. We are also being encouraged to eat less red meat and to substitute white meats, such as fish and chicken, and some vegetable proteins, such as nuts and beans. We are being encouraged to eat more whole grains in bread, wheat, corn, and rice; to eat more fresh fruit and vegetables and to eat more of these uncooked. A healthy balance is developing around these ideas. The changes are taking place gradually and are no longer seen as the ideas of an affluent minority in the "health food" lobby. They are affecting the whole population as food processors and retailers realize that there is a widespread public demand for such changes. They have been helped in this by the actions of some school boards, as in New York, where public policy has actively promoted such changes with what have been suggested are improvements in pupils' health and scholastic achievement.

Yet, in the debate about the introduction of food irradiation, there has been hardly any consideration of the impact of the process on the diet. The very foods we are being encouraged to eat more of—white meats such as chicken and fish, whole grains, and fresh fruit and vegetables—are the target foods for irradiation, and all of them could suffer losses in some essential nutrients as a result.

## Vitamins

It is not in dispute that irradiation causes damage to many vitamins. Vitamin A, vitamins $B_1$ (thiamine), $B_2$, $B_3$, $B_6$, $B_{12}$, folic acid, vitamin C (ascorbic acid), and vitamins E and K are all damaged to a greater or lesser extent by irradiation (Table 8). Essential polyunsaturated fatty acids (PUFAs) are also affected. These are increasingly being valued for their contribution to health

### Table 8: Some Reported Percentage Vitamin Losses From Irradiation

| Food | Vitamin A | B$_1$ | B$_2$ | B$_3$ | B$_6$ | B$_{12}$ | C | E |
|---|---|---|---|---|---|---|---|---|
| Milk | 60-70 | 35-85 | 24-74 | 33 | 15-21 | 31-33 | | 40-60 |
| Butter | 51-78 | | | | | | | |
| Cheese | 32-47 | | | | | | | |
| Grains and flour | | | | | | | | |
| Wheat | — | 20-63 | — | 15 | 3 | — | — | — |
| Oats | | 35-86 | | | | | | 7-45 |
| Rice | | 22 | | | | | | |
| Beans | — | | 48 | — | 48 | — | — | — |
| Meats | | | | | | | | |
| Beef | 43-76* | 42*-84* | 8-17* | — | 21*-25* | — | — | — |
| Pork and ham | 18* | 96* | 2* | 15* | 10-45* | | | |
| Chicken | 53-95* | 46-93* | 35*-38* | | 32*-37* | | | |
| Eggs | — | 24-61* | — | 18 | — | — | — | 17 |
| Fish | | | | | | | | |
| Cod | — | 47 | 2* | — | — | — | — | — |
| Haddock | | 70*-90* | 4* | | 26 | | | |
| Mackerel | | 15-85* | | | | | | |
| Shrimp | 2-27 | 70*-90* | | | | | | |
| Potatoes | — | — | — | — | — | — | 28-56 | — |
| Fruits | | | | | | | | |
| Fruit juices | — | — | — | — | — | — | 20-70 | — |
| Nuts | — | — | — | — | — | — | — | 19-32 |

Note some vitamins are relatively undamaged by radiation, but absence of a figure in the table above does not imply that a food has been cleared. In general, more work needs to be done on a comprehensive study of vitamin losses.
*All losses are at doses below the 10 kGy proposed clearance level unless *. In these cases, doses are below the 60 kGy being suggested for sterilization of meat products (Sources: References 13, 14, 15.)

as well as for the general benefits of substituting unsaturated for saturated fats. Vitamin E, which is known to be a protector of the PUFAs, is so badly damaged that in many cases it is even destroyed if it is put back into the food as an additive.

The extent of the loss depends on the vitamin, on the type of food, and on the dose of radiation given. Generally speaking, the more complex the food, the less it suffers vitamin losses during irradiation. Fruit juices suffer more than fresh fruits, and fruits more than vegetables, grains, and meat products. Nevertheless, as the table shows, losses of 20 to 80% are not uncommon, and there are still many gaps in the available scientific data on vitamin losses.[14,15,16]

## Public Health Implications?

Folic acid (folate) is an essential vitamin from the group of B vitamins. In its brief and inadequate discussion of the issue, the British ACINF said that "little is known about the effects of irradiation on folate." Since there are possible problems in the area of public health in relation to the intake of folic acid, this needs further investigation. Deficiencies in folic acid and in other vitamins[3] and minerals[4] have been linked to the development of neural tube defects such as spina bifida. In addition, studies of elderly people and people entering mental hospitals have found that a significant proportion of such people have deficiencies in folic acid.

The United States is unique in having high recommended daily allowances (RDAs) for most vitamins. The European RDA for vitamin C is about half that in the United States, mainly because the average daily intake in northern Europe does not meet the United States standard. In Britain, a recent report from the Department of Health and Social Security found major deficiencies in the diet of British schoolchildren.[5] In many parts of the United States, particularly among those whose diet is limited by lack of adequate income, there are groups of people whose diet is already deficient.[6]

The same would apply to a much greater extent in less developed countries. Unfortunately, food irradiation advocates see nothing but benefits from irradiation in the war on hunger and malnutrition. The dream rapidly turns into a nightmare if we think that irradiation may be used to extend the storage life of the developed world's mountains of surplus food, so that these nutritionally depleted stockpiles can be off-loaded onto third world countries—adding insult to injury by calling it "aid."

The fact is that this technology has been introduced with too little consideration of the impact it will have on diet. No studies anywhere have assessed whether there will be a significant impact either on the population as a whole or on vulnerable groups within the population.

The first response of many of the experts who have been asked to comment on this issue has been to argue that these losses are not likely to be significant. When the extent of the losses is pointed out to them, they say that it is within the normal range of losses that would occur naturally in cooking and storage. Since these normal losses vary between 0 and 100%, this is hardly surprising, but, in fact, the comparison is both untrue and misleading.

For example:

- Some irradiated foods are to be sold as fresh and, in some cases such as fruits and some vegetables, eaten fresh and raw. Consumers may assume they are getting full nutritional value when they are actually eating a vitamin-depleted processed food.
- Some vitamins, $B_1$ for example, undergo accelerated losses in storage if the food has been irradiated. As we noted earlier, vitamin E is virtually destroyed even if put back in as an additive.
- Irradiated food is intended to be stored longer, so nutrient storage losses will be greater.
- Irradiation and storage losses are then added to by losses in cooking and storing. Typical vitamin losses during household preparation of food are already significant, as Table 9 shows.

### Table 9: Average Vitamin Losses During Household Preparation of Foods (%)

| | |
|---|---|
| Thiamin | 30 |
| Riboflavin | 15 |
| Niacin | 20 |
| Ascorbic acid | 35 |
| Folic acid | 40-50 |

(Source: Reference 16.)

The food can thus undergo initial losses on irradiation, accelerated losses during storage, and additional losses because of longer storage times, and then lose further vitamins in cooking.

In Britain, where there has been a furious debate on the issue of vitamin losses, the irradiation lobby has used a fall-back argument when confronted with these facts. Sir Arnold Burgen, the chairman of the British ACINF, said that it would not be a problem because no one was likely to eat a significant portion of the total diet from irradiated foods.[7] We believe this comes dangerously close to saying that irradiated food is all right as long as you don't eat it!

At an earlier meeting with the British Food and Drink Federation, an industry spokesperson challenged us to name any food that was likely to be both irradiated and consumed in significant quantity. We suggested that the British were known world-wide for their consumption of fish and chips—and there was a rapid change of subject. Given that irradiation is considered appropriate for some fresh fruits and for potatoes, fish, and chicken, it is clear that some staple foods could be affected.

In a final attempt to defuse the public outcry, the British ACINF suggested that there should be long-term monitoring of irradiated food for nutritional damage. It would, we suggest, be better for such research to be done *before* the widespread application of irradiation to food, not after. As with the area of food safety, the opinions of the expert committee are no substitute for scientific evidence. It should also be noted that many of the adverse effects noted in the chapter on food safety could be caused by vitamin deficiencies in the diet of the experimental animals. In the absence of hard evidence on nutritional changes, the widespread consumption of irradiated food would be an uncontrolled human experiment.

## Counterfeiting Freshness?

Irradiated foods look fresh longer. The consumer will be encouraged to view them as healthy and wholesome, whereas they are likely to be older and more depleted in essential health constituents. In these circumstances, the potential for deceit—for what can best be described as "counterfeiting" fresh food—is considerable.

In many consumer surveys that have been done around the world,[8,9,10,11] people have consistently demanded that irradiated food be labeled. For some, this simply represents a desire to know that the food has been treated in this way so that they are not misled. For others, the demand will clearly enable them to avoid these foods. For still others, it may be that they will see benefits in irradiation for which they are prepared to pay a premium price. And for some, there will be a need to know so that they do not, in fact, have too great a portion of the diet irradiated—at least until the full dietary impact of irradiation has been adequately assessed.

Consumers know that food purchased in cans has been processed, and that foods from the grocery freezer have been frozen, so they must balance their diets for any vitamin losses caused by processing. If they try to compensate with foods from the fresh produce department and purchase secretly irradiated items, the nutritional balancing act will fail.

Yet, despite these valid reasons for having irradiated food clearly labeled as such, there has been a remarkable reluctance on the part of the authorities, the pro-irradiation lobby, and the food industry to allow labeling to be done simply and honestly. The 1984 FDA-proposed rule for irradiating fruits and vegetables tried to drop the existing labeling requirement. FDA officials stated that Margaret Heckler's office removed their initial recommendation for consumer labeling.[12] The no-label proposal elicited several thousand letters demanding that irradiated foods be labeled, although most writers preferred that the process not be approved.

In the United States, companion bills have been introduced in the House and Senate that would prevent individual states from enacting their own legislation to require labeling. In one of her last acts before resigning as Secretary of Health and Human Services, Margaret Heckler announced that the label would contain the term "picowaved," probably as an attempt to draw on the widespread acceptance of microwave technology, even though microwaves cannot alter the food chemistry as ionizing radiation can. Fortunately, this idea didn't pass the "laugh test" within the corridors of power. The FDA's final rule (April 18, 1986) requires labeling of whole foods with the statement "treated with radiation" or "treated by irradiation," and the use of a symbol that looks like a stamp of approval. Unfortunately for consumers in the United States, the requirement to label foods with words that tell us what has been done to it will be dropped in April 1988, and food manufacturers may then be free to use only the symbol.

The United States symbol is similar to the "Radura" label that was first developed for use in South Africa and the Netherlands. American consumer activists charge that the symbol is misleading. They think that the stylized flower inside a circle is more suggestive of a health food than an irradiated one. The Environmental Protection Agency pointed out the close similarity of the symbol to its own logo (Figure 3).

The system in Europe is in fact voluntary. It is very hard to find any food with this label on it in Europe. The Dutch irradiators tell us that all their food goes for export. The South Africans, no doubt fearful of fueling the boycott of South African produce, assure us that none of theirs is exported, though there is evidence of a test marketing trial of South African produce in the Netherlands in 1984.

In Britain, the ACINF reluctantly recommended that irradiated food be labeled—just as well, because a national opinion poll conducted for the London Food Commission showed that 95% of the public thought that all irradiated foods, including ingredients of processed foods, should be clearly labeled as irradiated. The use of the words "the emblem of quality" would almost certainly contravene the United Kingdom's Trade Descriptions Act, which prohibits any false claims in advertising. What is clearly needed is international agreement for clear and unambiguous labeling of all irradiated foods as "irradiated."

Even this will not be enough. Within Europe, the European Commission is the body that actually drafts the laws that will be applied by all European governments; the elected European Parliament has only an advisory role at present. The Commission is currently considering a draft directive that would not require labeling of any food making up less than 5% by weight of the finished product. Furthermore, this directive would require all governments to pass laws no more restrictive of irradiation than those of the directive. The states' rights issue in the United States is paralleled by loss of sovereign rights for European nations through the determination of the irradiation lobby to conceal, as far as possible, the fact that food has been irradiated.

There are considerable pressures in Europe for nutritional labeling, at least at the minimum level that exists in the United States, where the vitamin and other nutritional values of foods are printed on the package. More and better labeling is in fact needed. The information is currently given in as unintelligible a form as manufacturers are permitted to provide. How do food manufacturers intend to modify the nutritional label to take account of vitamin losses?

As we have seen, irradiated food is intended to be stored longer.

Environmental Protection Agency Logo

The Radura Label in the UK and South Africa

The Radura Label
required by the US FDA

Consumer organizations urge that irradiated foods should
be labeled "Irradiated" or "Treated with Ionizing Radiation."

**Figure 3 Labeling of Irradiated Foods**

Wherever they have been asked, consumers indicate that they want the date of irradiation to be stamped on the food so that they will know how old it is.[8] The food industry has been able to gain acceptance for the vague "sell by" date marking system. Is a return to a more honest date marking system a price that the industry is prepared to pay for the benefits it expects to get from irradiation?

## Food Quality—and Food Prices

There is really no economic advantage to a food processing company in irradiating the best quality food and thus having to add on the cost of irradiation to the price. There is, however, considerable economic advantage to irradiating lower-quality food so that it stays looking fresh—like the high-quality food it counterfeits—for longer. This food can then be sold so as to marginally undercut the high-quality product. This is not a hypothetical concern. Already, importers of high-quality herbs and spices in Europe are concerned that irradiation may be used by their competitors to "clean up" cheaper, low-quality spices from southern Europe and North Africa, and so undercut the high-quality products they currently buy from the United States. The spice market in the United States may soon be forced to accept irradiation—and lower quality standards—in order to remain competitive. Does anyone benefit from this?

Labeling is therefore a much wider issue than merely preserving the right of individual consumers to know food has been irradiated, and then to be left at the mercy of the powerful food industry's ability to manipulate prices, to alter public perceptions through advertising, and to conceal what has really been done to the food. In the final analysis, labeling is about giving the consumer some control over food quality in the increasingly international marketplace for food. It is also, in the absence of any studies on the impact of irradiation on the diet, a public health issue. People need to know when food has been irradiated so as to be able to balance the diet with high-quality fresh foods. We need to be assured that if irradiation is to be used, there will be full disclosure of relevant information and the maintenance of the highest quality standards.

REFERENCES

1. *Nutrition and Your Health: Dietary Guidelines for Americans.* US Department of Agriculture and US Department of Health and Human Services, 1985.
2. National Advisory Committee on Nutrition Education, Health Education Council 1983; COMA Diet and Cardiovascular Disease. London: HMSO, 1984.
3. R. W. Smithells, et al. Further Experience of Vitamin Supplementation for Prevention of Neural Tube Defect Recurrences. *Lancet,* 1027-1031, 1983.
4. M. H. Soltan and D. M. Jenkins. Maternal and Foetal Plasma Zinc Concentration and Foetal Abnormality. *British Journal of Obstetrics and Gynaecology,* 89, 56-58, 1982.
5. R. W. Wenlock, et al. *The Diets of British Schoolchildren.* DHSS. London: HMSO, 1986.
6. Hearing of the US Senate Select Committee on Hunger, Washington, DC, April 4, 1986, and Michael F. Jacobson. *The Complete Eater's Digest and Nutritional Scoreboard.* Garden City, NY: Anchor/Doubleday, 1986.
7. Sir Arnold Burgen. Statement to DHSS Press Conference, London, April 10, 1986.
8. Titlebaum, Dubin, and Doyle. Will Consumers Accept Irradiated Foods. *Journal of Food Safety,* 5, 219-228, 1983, and Bruhn, Schultz, and Sommer. Attitude Change Toward Food Irradiation Among Conventional and Alternative Consumers. Vol. 40, *Food Technology,* 86, January 1986.
9. Survey conducted by the UK Consumers' Association, London, November 1986.
10. *Food Irradiation.* Omnibus Research by Marplan Ltd. Conducted for the London Food Commission, London, January 1987.
11. Brand Group. *Irradiated Seafood Products: A Position Paper for the Seafood Industry.* Prepared for the National Marine Fisheries Service, Washington, DC, January 1986.
12. Sanford Miller, FDA Center for Food Safety and Applied Administration, Statement at FDA Consumer Forum, Washington, DC, April 11, 1984.
13. Edward S. Josephson and Martin S. Peterson, eds. *Preservation of Food by Ionizing Radiation* (3 vols.). Florida: CRC Press, Vol. 1 1982, Vols. 2 & 3 1983.
14. P. S. Elias and A. J. Cohen. *Recent Advances in Food Irradiation.* Amsterdam and New York: Elsevier Biomedical Press, 1983.
15. P. S. Elias and A. J. Cohen. *Radiation Chemistry of Major Food Components.* Amsterdam and New York: Elsevier Biomedical Press, 1977.
16. W. Heiman. *Fundamentals of Food Chemistry.* Chichester, England: Ellis Horwood, 1980.

# CHAPTER 5

# CAN FOOD IRRADIATION BE CONTROLLED?

LET US ASSUME for the moment that irradiated food is safe, that consumers welcome the benefits it offers, and that they are willing to pay a premium price for food that keeps longer and is guaranteed free of food-poisoning organisms. What is there to stop the unscrupulous trader from labeling food "irradiated" that has never gone near an irradiation plant? The answer is, incredibly, nothing! There is currently no test that can be used to show that a food has been irradiated. There is no test to show what dose it has received or how many times it has been irradiated.

Perhaps more worrying, however, is that there are also no tests to show what may have gone on inside the food before it was irradiated.

As we have seen, there are doubts over the safety and wholesomeness of irradiated foods; but even if there were not, we need to be assured that it can be controlled—that we have the system of regulations, agencies, trained staff, and technology to ensure that it is used properly. None of this exists.

In 1986 it was revealed that a company in one of Britain's major food groups, Imperial Foods, had used irradiation to conceal bacterial contamination of seafoods that were then sold for public consumption in Britain.[1,2]

It was revealed that the British Imperial Foods Group subsidiary, Young's Seafoods (now owned by the United States/United Kingdom financial giant, the Hanson Trust), had used irradiation to conceal contamination of seafoods that were then sold for public consumption in England, where irradiation and sale of irradiated food is illegal.[2] The company found contamination on a shipment of prawns that it had imported into Britain. It shipped these prawns to the Netherlands for irradiation and then, illegally, reimported these same prawns back into Britain to be sold under the "Admiral" label (See Appendix 2).[2]

This is not an isolated case. A television program, "4 What It's Worth," produced for the British Channel 4 network, also reported that the Flying Goose Company, now part of the British Allied Lyons Group (which owns food companies in the United States such as Baskin-Robbins), had sent prawns to the IRE irradiation plant in Belgium to be irradiated.[3] These prawns were sent to Sweden, where, as in Britain, the importation of irradiated food is prohibited.[3] The company was reported as saying that the shipment had been a mistake and the practice would not continue. However, the consignment was rejected by the customer in Sweden following a tip-off. The Swedish authorities allowed it to be re-exported. Its final destination was unknown.[4]

Irradiation has been used on spices that have been sent to West Germany and irradiation was used on a shipment of contaminated mussels that was sent to Denmark. Like the Imperial Group's prawns, these foods were irradiated at the Gammaster plant in The Netherlands.[5]

The International Maritime Bureau is investigating cases of possible insurance fraud involving shipments of various foods to the United States. It is believed that shipments of seafood and frogs' legs may have been overinsured before being rejected by the authorities in the United States. Once the insurance claims are made, the consignments are then bought back as "reject lots" and shipped to Europe for irradiation before being put back on the market. One consignment of frogs' legs is suspected of having crossed the Atlantic 11 times.

When asked to take legal action to stop these abuses, the British government minister replied that it was a matter for the port authorities and that, in any case, one documented example did not indicate widespread abuse.[6]

Our information is that the practice of concealing bacterial contamination by use of irradiation is more widespread than the governments are prepared to admit, partly because they are unable to control it. Seafood products such as those just described travel the world as relatively valuable consignments. Within the trade, their whereabouts is fairly well known. These cases also involve illegal trade and so have been easier to track down. These documented cases represent the tip of the iceberg. Many other irradiated products are similarly traded. If the current bans in these European countries were removed in the absence of stringent controls, such abuses would be even more frequent.

The reason for concern goes beyond legality and beyond even the deceit involved in concealing bacterial contamination. Irradiation can reduce the bacterial load on foods—known in the trade as the "bug count"—but it leaves unaffected the toxins generated by the earlier bacterial contamination, which can present a very real public health hazard.

The FAO/IAEA/WHO Joint Expert Committee emphasized that irradiation should be used only to extend the shelf life of otherwise wholesome food and should never be used to make unfit food saleable.[7] Yet this is precisely what is already happening in countries where irradiation is permitted, and is even occurring, despite the law, in countries where it is not.

When consumers, public health agencies, or responsible food companies inspect food for its wholesomeness and saleability, we use our eyes to see if it looks fresh and our nose to see if it smells bad; if in doubt, we can send it to the laboratory for a "bug count." Unfortunately, irradiation is intended to make food look fresh longer, kill the bacteria that cause it to smell bad, and kill most of the bacteria that are usually detected in the bug count.

Use of irradiation makes all the usual testing systems for food wholesomeness ineffective. A whole new battery of tests will be needed just to determine whether foods have been irradiated. There will also be a need for appropriate training of the staff involved in monitoring for food safety. There has been massive funding for research designed to show that irradiated food is "safe." Until very recently, there has been no funding of research into methods of detecting irradiation treatment.[8] Without such methods, it will be impossible to provide assurances—in the real world of the international food trade—about the safety of possibly irradiated foods.

A survey conducted in Britain revealed that there had been no preparation of the responsible agencies—port health and trading standards officers—for monitoring, detection, and control of irradiated foods.[9] Not only are there no available tests to detect irradiation, there are no readily available tests for measuring many of the chemical toxins directly if concealment of earlier contamination by irradiation is suspected. Even those toxin tests that do exist are complicated and expensive, and would not be used routinely.

The United States National Bureau of Standards and a British university have recently begun to collaborate on research that may lead to a battery of tests being available, perhaps within the next three years. At the time of writing, one of them involves detection of small changes in the level of some protein chemicals, such as ortho-tyrosine in meats. Another is designed to identify residual free radicals in hard foods, e.g., in bone or chitin, using electronic spin resonance techniques. This may also be useful for other dry whole foods. Other approaches based on changes in food chemistry, chemiluminescence, measurement of electrical conductivity in foods such as potatoes, or measurement of differentials between bacterial and toxin counts and detection of changes in the DNA—that part of the food's chemistry that carries the genetic code—are also under consideration. As yet, none of these approaches is developed to the point where public health agencies or concerned companies can use them to detect irradiation. It will take considerably longer to develop tests that measure the dose of radiation received or how many times a food has been reirradiated before being sold to the consumer.

What we find amazing is that there is, as yet, no serious government funding for this research. The United States/United Kingdom research program described here is partly funded by charitable donations from the British company Ken Bell International. Ken Bell has been an outspoken critic of irradiation and the major source of information on current abuses in the irradiated food trade.[3]

Perhaps most incredible of all is the fact that various governments, that of the United States included, have given permits for irradiation without there being a regulatory, testing, and enforcement system in place and without appropriation of significant funds for the research to develop tests that could help stamp out the abuses that are going on. The United Kingdom Ministry of Agriculture, Fisheries, and Food has allowed only £150,000 a year for research in this area.[8]

Whatever the views on the safety of long-term consumption of irradiated foods, many responsible companies in the food industry have given assurances that they will respect the consumers' demand for labeling of all irradiated foods. Unfortunately, without tests to detect irradiation, they cannot guarantee that some unscrupulous supplier has not used irradiation at some stage. There seems to be common ground between the food industry and consumers for a moratorium on irradiation until such tests are available and until monitoring, control, and enforcement systems are developed. The few years of breathing space would allow time to clear up the confusion over safety testing and other concerns about irradiated foods. This position has been adopted by the British Food and Drink Federation[10] and endorsed by the European Parliament.[11]

For the moment, however, we are dependent on the integrity of the irradiation companies, processors, shippers, and retailers to measure, record, and provide documentation on irradiated foods all the way down the line from the irradiation plants to the consumer, if we are to know anything about their history. Such documentary approaches are inadequate. The USDA, for all its inspections and controls, uncovered only one illegal shipment of irradiated pork on its way to Sweden when the ship was in the mid-Atlantic.[12] The idea that irradiation companies will take the trouble to inquire about a food's history and final destination before irradiating it flies in the face of the evidence.[3,4] Sources in the food trade report that European brokers openly offer to have consignments irradiated and some traders regularly deal in "reject" consignments.

So far, however, governments have refused to take action against the companies involved in abusing irradiation or to stop the abuses. How many more cases must we and other independent researchers uncover (and provide the hard-to-obtain documentary evidence for) before our governments will take action?

## Working with Radiation

The abuse of food safety, unfortunately, is only one of the areas where we have reason to doubt that the irradiation industry will act with integrity. Exposure of food to radiation may, in the end, have some beneficial effects. Exposure of workers has none.

Large doses of radiation can kill by destroying cells in the body so that various organs cease to function, or by damaging the body's immune system, leaving it susceptible to disease. Some acute effects such as skin burn, nausea, and diarrhea are also experienced; they may not cause death, but years later, exposed people may suffer from cancer, or their children from genetic damage, as a result of the exposure. Even at doses too low to bring about immediate effects, there remains an increased risk of cancer, genetic damage, or susceptibility to disease.[13,14,15,16]

There is no threshold or safe level. When radiation strikes a living cell, one of three things can occur:

- Damage done, if any, is adequately repaired.
- The cell is killed. In this case, provided too many cells are not killed at once, the body will eliminate the dead cells and little harm will be done.
- The cell will be damaged but survive to reproduce in this damaged form. Years later, successive reproductions from the damaged cell may show up as what we call a tumor or cancer, or be passed on as a genetic defect to future generations.[15,17]

Also, a growing body of evidence suggests that radiation causes a more general reduction in health by weakening the body's resistance to disease.[15,17]

The crucial point is that there is no dose below which these effects do not occur. It is like walking across a main road blindfolded. Do this at rush hour and you'll probably be killed. Do it at midnight when there is less traffic and you may be more lucky; but if you are hit by one of the few vehicles around you will be just as dead. A little bit of radiation does not give you a little bit of cancer. Any dose, however small, can be the one that does the damage[15] that, years later, may show up as cancer or other health problems in this or future generations.

The extremely large doses involved in the irradiation of food could result in exposure to workers in the industry. They face considerable risks in the event of malfunctioning equipment, leaking radioactive sources, or accidental exposure to the source. In addition, the irradiation chamber will be a very corrosive atmosphere requiring "regular and preventative maintenance."[13] Irradiation sources will also need to be produced, transported, stored, and installed, and the spent sources replaced. At every stage workers can be, and usually are, exposed to "low levels" of radiation.[19]

As a general principle, any exposure to radiation should be

avoided unless it can be justified in terms of some overall benefit. Even then, the exposure should be kept as low as possible.[12,20] In addition, there are regulations setting limits on the maximum dose that workers and/or the public can be exposed to. Unfortunately, most of these regulations were set before establishment of the principle that there is no safe level. As a result, most radiation use technologies developed under standards that can now be seen as inadequate. It is, however, very costly both in economic terms, and, more importantly, in terms of the safety image of these industries, to admit the error. Considerable effort, which could be better spent on radiation protection for workers and the public, has gone into attempting to maintain the myth that exposures within the limits are "acceptable."

A person is permitted to receive a maximum of 5 rem per year external whole body exposure to radiation at work, or a maximum of 0.5 rem as a member of the public, with certain exceptions. A rem (roentgen equivalent man) is a measure of the biological damage done by radiation. For gamma radiation, electron beams, and x-rays, it is effectively the same as the rad used to measure doses to food.

As with rad and Gy, the Sievert has now replaced the rem in most countries except the United States. Since the Sievert is a large dose compared with the likely worker dose, the milliSievert (mSv) is commonly used (0.001 Sievert); 1 rem equals 10 mSv.

The 5 rem (50mSv) limit was set in 1957. Since then, it has become clear that exposure to this level of radiation represents a completely unacceptable level of risk, using the officially accepted levels of risk from radiation. A worker receiving this dose each year would run a risk eight times higher than is acceptable for a "safe" industry, and more than double the risk faced by workers in high-risk jobs such as mining.[21,22,23] A "safe industry" accepts that one worker in 10,000 will die each year; or, over a lifetime, one in 200 workers will die from an accident at work. Clearly, a risk eight or more times greater than this is completely unacceptable.

For a worker to face radiation risks equal to risks in a "safe industry," the exposure limit will need to be reduced to about 0.5 rem (5 mSv) a year. Even then, radiation workers will face all the normal risks of other accidents and so will still be doubling their risk of dying from the job.[24]

On top of this, these risks apply only to fatal cancers and serious genetic damage over two generations. The nonfatal but debilitating effects of other cancers, the less serious or long-term genetic effects, and the general lowering of the quality of health from radiation should not be forgotten.

The need for a drastic reduction of the dose limits, by at least a factor of 10, is reinforced by the more recent scientific evidence on the risks of radiation exposure. The national standards and the risk estimates are usually based on the recommendations of the International Commission on Radiological Protection (ICRP), a self-appointed body of experts closely identified with the nuclear industry.[14,25] Two recent international reviews of the scientific literature have put the risks between two and 10 times higher than does the ICRP.[26,27]

Further evidence suggests that the risks may be higher still.[28, 29,30,31,32] Studies of Japanese survivors of the atomic bombings in 1945 show a higher-than-expected incidence of cancer, and the dose of radiation they received is less than was previously believed.

The most recent evidence from studies of nuclear workers in the United States and the United Kingdom indicates that the risk is probably four to six times, but could be as much as 15 times, greater than estimates by the ICRP.[32]

## New Regulations?

In these circumstances it might have been expected that the changes to regulations being considered by the United States Nuclear Regulatory Commission (NRC)[33] and by almost all other countries would have revised and improved standards for radiation protection. Unfortunately, the reverse is the case. In some significant ways, these new regulations relax the already inadequate standards currently in force.[22,34]

Under the new ICRP-based system for calculating worker doses from exposure to different parts of the body, the permitted dose to a number of organs is to be allowed to rise by two to eight times the current limits (See Table 10).

**Table 10: Current and proposed limits for organ exposures**

| Organ | Old limit (rem) | New limit (rem) | Factor increase |
|---|---|---|---|
| Thyroid | 30 | 50 | 1.7 × |
| Breast | 15 | 32 | 2.1 × |
| Bone | 30 | 50 | 1.7 × |
| Red marrow | 5 | 42 | 8.4 × |
| Lung | 15 | 42 | 2.8 × |
| Gonads | 5 | 20 | 4.0 × |
| Skin | 30 | 50 | 1.7 × |
| Extremities | 75 | 50 | 0.67 × |
| Head (in some circumstances) | | | 3.0 × |

(Source: Reference 20, 34, 38.)

Most of the limits on amounts of particular radioactive materials that a worker can absorb are also relaxed, in some cases quite dramatically.[22]

These relaxations are taking place despite the private view of many within even the nuclear establishment that exposures need to be below 1 rem (10 mSv) to be considered acceptable.[35]

## Are Design Standards for Food Irradiation Plants Adequate?

Clearly, in these circumstances, food irradiation technology will be introduced into a regulatory framework that does not provide adequate protection for radiation workers. Once established, the technology will be yet one more reason why improvements cannot be made in the future. It will undoubtedly then be argued that changes will cost money and jobs.

Several eminent scientists in the field of radiation protection have argued for a new limit for radiation technology of 0.5 rem (5 mSv), which should be the maximum a worker is likely to receive from all normal operations involving exposure to radiation.[36,37] Unions in the United Kingdom and Canada have called for a phased reduction of all radiation exposures to below this limit.[38,39] The need for lower limits was recently endorsed by the International Chemical and Energy Federation, representing most of the western world's unions in this field.[40]

For most purposes, a 0.5 rem (5 mSv) limit is already feasible.[19,21,41] In the case of a new technology such as food irradiation, the plant can be designed to ensure that the limit is not exceeded.

These measures will not, as already indicated, remove all risks, but they would begin to bring these risks into line with those faced in other industries. Just like consumers, workers need to be allowed to make informed choices about the risks and to have adequate protection laid down by a framework of regulations.

Lest these concerns be thought of as peripheral, it should be noted that in 1986, the NRC revoked the license on the Rockaway food irradiation plant of Radiation Technology, Inc., for violations of worker health and safety regulations that could have caused serious overexposure of some of the workforce.[42] The NRC concluded that the violations

> . . . were wilful and that numerous management and operations personnel wilfully provided false information to the NRC thus demonstrating a pattern of wrongdoing so pervasive that the NRC no longer has reasonable assurances . . . that the licensee will comply with NRC requirements and that public health and safety will be protected. If at the time the license was issued the NRC had known that such a pattern would develop the license would not have been issued.[43]

Radiation Technology, Inc., has been cited 32 times for various violations, including throwing radioactive garbage out with the regular trash.[44] The most serious violation involved bypassing an interlock safety device that prevents people from entering the irradiation cell during operation.[45] In 1977, one worker received a near lethal dose of radiation.[44] The NRC investigation found that Dr. Martin Welt, the company's founder and president, ordered that the interlock system be bypassed and that he and other senior managers directed employees to give false information on the matter to the NRC investigators.[43]

Under pressure from the NRC, Martin Welt resigned as president but retained his stockholding in the firm and will continue to do planning and consulting work for it.[46] The Department of Energy has appointed Dr. Welt to a job, at $100 per hour plus expenses, as advisor to the advisory committee to plan the six DOE-funded demonstration irradiation plants.[46]

The Radiation Technology worker over exposure is not an isolated case. An Isomedix worker received a dose of about 400 rads when he entered the radiation chamber in Parsippany, New Jersey, on June 13, 1974. The worker received a dose considered lethal for 70% of people so exposed, but prompt hospital treatment helped save his life, and he was discharged from the hospital on July 27, 1974.[47]

## Environmental Safety and Controls

Many workers live close to their jobs. They and the rest of the community face particular hazards from the operation of the plant and the transport in and out of the highly radioactive sources used.

Coverups have also been alleged at other irradiation companies. A nine-count federal indictment issued on June 24, 1986, charged International Nutronics and company officials Eugene T. O'Sullivan and Bruce J. Thomas with the coverup of a radioactive spill in December 1982.[48] International Nutronics formerly operated a radiation sterilization plant in Dover, New Jersey. On December 4, 1982, International Nutronics employees found several inches of radioactive water covering the floor of the plant because a hose had blown out and was leaking radioactive water from a pool that stored cobalt 60.[49] Approximately 600 gallons of contaminated water leaked from a pool that held about 500,000 curies of cobalt 60 when the source was not in use. The water in the cobalt 60 pool was contaminated as early as 1974 by one or more broken cobalt 60 sources.[50]

Company officials ordered workers to clean up the spill without protective equipment, and some of the water was carried in buckets to a shower stall and dumped down a drain into the Dover sewer system. Workers were not given proper protective clothing during the internal cleanup, and they were asked to move radiation badges from belt level up to their collars so that the badges would not reveal the true level of their radiation doses.[51] Contaminated water was poured down the shower stalls into the sewer system in violation of requirements to ship contaminated water to a radioactive waste site. Company officials did not inform the NRC of the accident, as required by regulations, and by the time the NRC learned of it about 10 months later through a whistle-blowing worker, radioactive contamination was found outside the building.[52] The plant is located in a densely populated area, within 100 feet of both residences and a major highway.[53]

Records of the operation of a demonstration food irradiator in Hawaii and radiation sterilizers owned by Isomedix and Radiation Technology offer further evidence of leakage problems in cobalt 60 plants. The Hawaii development irradiator was established by the Atomic Energy Commission and the Hawaii State Department of Agriculture in 1967 to research papaya irradiation. The first shipment of cobalt 60 arrived from Brookhaven National Laboratories in 1967. It was discovered that the source was leaking after it was installed in the storage pool inside the building. They dropped a shipping cask through the roof plug opening into the source pool to retrieve the damaged source. The source pool water contaminated the outside of the shipping cask, and the radioactive water dripped onto the roof, spreading the contamination. Despite some efforts to clean up the site, during which the machine room, tools, and workers' clothing became contaminated, problems persisted.

The facility operated until 1973, when funds were no longer available, and eventually the cobalt 60 source was removed and transferred to the University of Hawaii. The Hawaiian legislature allocated $385,000 to decontaminate the facility and convert it for other use in 1979. A contractor discovered cobalt 60 contamination on the lawn at the site on March 23, 1980. Experts believe that at one meter from the contaminated area of lawn, approximately six by eight feet, a person would have been exposed to the equivalent of 7.5 chest radiographs per hour. The public was apparently at risk for many years from the original accidental releases in 1967.[54]

Isomedix, Inc. had another leaking cobalt 60 source in 1976,[55] and Radiation Technology was fined by the NRC for a leaking cobalt 60 source whose endcap loosened in 1975. It had been sealed in a pipe and stored at the bottom of the pool.[56] Despite industry claims, cobalt 60 sources can and do leak.

Isomedix, the largest radiation sterilizing company in the United States, has been cited by the NRC for allegedly (a) overexposing workers to radiation, (b) failing to post radiation areas, (c) allowing food and cigarettes in the same areas as radioactive materials, (d) operating the facility without authorized personnel physically present, and (e) failing to adequately monitor the water disposed into sanitary sewage systems.[57,58] The last violation was discovered when former workers advised the NRC that Isomedix had conducted unsafe practices, such as disposing of contaminated water from the cobalt 60 pool by dumping it into a toilet connected to the public sewer system. The NRC verified that a pipe leading from a toilet was measurably contaminated in 1979.[58]

Other radiation sterilization plants have suffered fires in the irradiation rooms. In one case, at Becton Dickinson, a product fell off the conveyor, and when the heat of the source caused it to ignite, the automatic sprinkling system failed to extinguish the fire.[59]

In short, the history of the irradiation plants already in operation leaves much to be desired. What assurance can we have that operation of future plants will be better controlled?

---

REFERENCES

1. Irradiated Foods: Illegal Importation. Early Day Motion, House of Commons Order Paper, London, April 9, 1986.
2. Stephen Leather. We Broke Law with Gamma Ray Prawns, Say Food Firm. *Daily Mail* (London), March 3, 1986.
3. Thames T.V. to Channel 4, 4 What It's Worth. April 8, 1986.
4. Per Axel Janson. *Dagens Nyheter* (Stockholm, Sweden), August 6, 1986.
5. J. B. Nielsen. Danish firm is sending tainted mussels to Holland to be irradiated. *Information* (Copenhagen), February 3, 1987; O. Lindboe. Reporting of irradiated mussels. *Politiken* (Copenhagen), February 3, 1987; NOAH erstattet Anzeige gegen Roemoe Muslinge Kompagniet. *Der Nordschleswiger* (Aabenraa), February 3, 1987; T. B. Nielsen. Mussels for 600,000 DKr. are destroyed. *Vestkysten* (Esbjerg), Feburary 4, 1987; J. B. Nielsen. Will not destroy irradiated mussels. *Information* (Copenhagen), February 20, 1987; Fines are to be expected for irradiated mussels. *Aktuelt* (Copenhagen), February 25, 1987; T. B. Nielsen. Irradiated mussels on Roemoe are destructed. *Vestkysten* (Esbjerg), April 10, 1987; Beschluss. Bestrahlte Muscheln vernichten oder verfuttern. *Der Nordschleswiger* (Aabenraa), April 10, 1987; J. Toft. Irradiated common mussels. *NOAH-Bladet* (Copenhagen), No. 107, April 1987, pp. 9-10.

6. Letter from Peggy Fenner, Parliamentary Secretary to the Ministry of Agriculture, Fisheries and Food, to the Director of the London Food Commission, 1986.

7. World Health Organization. *Wholesomeness of Irradiated Food.* Report of Joint FAO/IAEA/WHO Expert Committee. WHO Technical Report Series No. 659, Geneva, 1981.

8. UK Ministry of Agriculture Fisheries and Food announcement of grants of £150,000 ($225,000) per year for development of tests to detect irradiation, March 13, 1987

9. Survey of Trading Standards Officers by London Borough of Haringey, 1986.

10. Statement of FDF President Ross Buckland, London, 24 February 1987.

11. Opinion of the European Parliament on Irradiation of Foodstuffs, Brussels, adopted April 10, 1987.

12. Information supplied by Dr. Engel, USDA, Washington, DC, December 1986.

13. Edward S. Josephson and Martin S. Peterson, eds. *Preservation of Food by Ionizing Radiation* (3 vols.). Florida: CRC Press, Vol. 1 1982, Vols. 2 & 3 1983.

14. John W. Gofman. *Radiation and Human Health.* San Francisco: Sierra Club Books, 1981.

15. See T. Webb and R. Collingwood. *Radiation and Health—a Graphic Guide.* London: Camden Press, 1987. *Radiation on the Job.* Tape Slide Presentation for Canadian Union of Public Employees. Radiation and Health Information Service, Ottawa, Canada, 1983. Also, C. Ryle, J. Garrion, T. Webb. *Radiation Your Health at Risk.* Radiation and Health Information Service, Cambridge, England, 1980.

16. R. Bertell. *No Immediate Danger—Prognosis for a Radioactive Earth.* London: The Women's Press, 1985.

17. K. Z. Morgan, in C. Ryle, J. Garrison, and T. Webb. *Radiation: Your Health at Risk.* Radiation and Health Information Service, Cambridge, England, 1980.

18. G. V. Dalrymple and M. L. Baker. X-ray Examination for Breast Cancer: Benefit versus Risk. In W. R. Hendee, ed. *Health Effects of Low Level Radiation.* Englewood Cliffs, New Jersey: Appleton-Century-Crofts, 1984.

19. J. S. Hughes and G. C. Roberts. The Radiation Exposure of the UK Population 1984 Review. The National Radiological Protection Board, NRPB-R173, 1984.

20. *Annals of the International Commission on Radiological Protection—ICRP Report 26.* Oxford, England: Pergamon Press, 1977.

21. US Environmental Protection Agency Office of Radiation Programs. *Proposed Federal Radiation Protection Guidance for Occupational Exposure.* EPA 520 4-81-003. Chilton, England: January 1981.

22. US Nuclear Regulatory Commission. *Standards for Protection Against Radiation.* Revision of 10 CFR, Part 20. Draft [7590-01] US NRC, January 1983.

23. *Limitation of Exposure to Ionizing Radiation—Explanatory Notes Relating to a Proposed Amendment of the Atomic Energy Control Regulations.* Consultative Document C-78 AECB. Ottawa, Canada, 14 November 1983.

24. Brief of the Ontario Hydro Employees Union to the Atomic Energy Control Board on Proposed changes to Regulations under the Atomic Energy Control Act. Toronto, Canada, OHEU, January 1984.

25. P. A. Green. *The Controversy over Low Dose Exposure to Ionising Radiations.* MSc Thesis in Occupational Health and Safety. The University of Aston in Birmingham. October 1984.

26. United Nations Scientific Committee on the Effects of Atomic Radiation. *Sources and Effects of Ionizing Radiation.* Report to the General Assembly. United Nations, New York, 1982.

27. Committee on the Biological Effects of Ionizing Radiation (BEIR III). *The Effects on Populations of Exposure to Low Levels of Ionizing Radiation.* US National Academy of Sciences, 1980.

28. R. Bertell. *Handbook for Estimating Health Effects from Exposure to Ionizing Radiation.* Institute of Concern for Public Health, Toronto, Ontario, Canada, 1984.

29. T. Mancuso, A. Stewart, G. Kneale. Radiation Exposures of Hanford Workers Dying from Cancer and Other Causes. *Health Physics,* Vol. 33, 365–385, 1977. See also *British Journal of Medicine,* Vol. 28, 156–166, 1981, and *Ambio,* Vol. 9, No. 2.

30. W. E. Loewe, E. Mendelsohn. *Neutron and Gamma Doses at Hiroshima and Nagasaki.* Lawrence Livermore Laboratories, 1981.

31. T. Wakabayashi, H. Kato, T. Ikeda, W. J. Schull. Studies of the Mortality of A-Bomb Survivors, Report 7-111. Incidence of Cancer in 1959–1978 Based on the Tumour Registry, Nagasaki. *Radiation Research,* 93, 112–146, 1983.

32. V. Beral, H. Inskip, P. Fraser, M. Booth, D. Coleman, G. Rose. Mortality of Employees of the United Kingdom Atomic Energy Authority 1946–1979. *British Medical Journal,* Vol. 291, August 1985. See also Study of BNFL Workers, 1986.

33. 51 Federal Register 1092, January 9, 1986 (amending 10 CFR part 20).

34. The Health and Safety Commission. *Ionising Radiation Regulations* 1985. London: HMSO, 1985.

35. Note for the Record of a Discussion with Dr. A. S. McLean and Other Senior Staff of NRPB on the Implications of ICRP Publication 26, at Risley on 19 July 1978. UKAEA, Harwell, England, September, 1978.

36. B. Lindell. Statement to Public Forum on Nuclear Power, Middletown, PA, 1983. Also B. Lindell, D. J. Beninson, F. D. Sowby. *International Radiation Protection Regulations: 5 Years Experience of ICRP.* Publication 26, IAEA International Conference on Nuclear Power Experience, IAEA-CN-42/15. Vienna, September 1982.

37. E. P. Radford. Statement Concerning Proposed Federal Radiation Protection Guidance for Occupational Exposures. Hearings of the US Environmental Protection Agency, Office of Radiation Programs, Washington, DC, 1981.

38. Submission of the Canadian Labour Congress to the Atomic Energy Control Board on Proposed Revisions to Regulations Under the Atomic Energy Control Act. Canadian Labour Congress, Ottawa, Canada. January 1984.

39. Evidence to the Sizewell Inquiry. General, Municipal, Boilermakers and Allied Trades Union, Claygate, England, 1984.

40. World Conference of Workers in Nuclear Industries of the International Federation of Chemical, Energy and General Workers Unions (ICEF), Toronto, Ontario, Canada, October 13-15, 1986.

41. Frank Ley. In: Irradiation of Food Becoming Accepted, by John Young. *The Times* (London), 31 January 1983.

42. K. Tucker. *Pork Irradiation to Control Trichinae.* Health and Energy Institute, Washington, DC, 1986.

43. 51. Federal Register 23612, June 30, 1986.

44. USNRC v. Radiation Technology, 519 Fed. Supp. 1266 (D.NJ 1981)

45. NRC Occupational Radiation Exposure: Tenth Annual Report, 1977, NUREG-0463, 1978, pp. 17, 43, 110.

46. Robin Lally. NRC Removes Him, DOE Gets Him. *Daily Record* (Morris West, NJ), September 25, 1986, B1.

47. Atomic Energy Commission. Letter to John G. Davis from George Smith, dated July 31, 1974.

48. Wyckoff & Osay. Businessmen Charged in Cover-up of 1982 Radioactive Spill in Dover. *Daily Record* (Morris West, NJ), June 25, 1986. *American Health,* March 1987, p. 142.

49. USNRC Order Modifying License of International Nutronics, License No. 29-13848-01, dated November 1, 1983.

50. NRC print-out of accidents, item No. 82-0216, reported October 25, 1982.

51. Wyckoff. Surprise for Radiation Workers. *Daily Record* (Morris West, NJ), June 26, 1986.

52. USNRC Order Modifying License Effective Immediately of International Nutronics, License No. 29-13848-01, Washington, DC, January 30, 1984.

53. USNRC Response to Questions Concerning Immediately Effective Order Issued to International Nutronics, Inc., dated June 14, 1984.

54. Letter from Alexander M. Dollar, Supervisor, Hawaii Development Irradiator, to Herbert Brook, AEC, April 5, 1967. Letter from Ralph M. Baltzo to Yukio Kitagawa, Hawaii Department of Agriculture, June 9, 1980. Food Irradiation Response, Radiological Contamination and Hazard at the Hawaiian Developmental Irradiator, 1968 through 1980. Factsheet received by HEI from Food Irradiation Response, 1986.

55. George Dietz, President, Isomedix. Letter to USNRC, dated August 11, 1976.

56. USNRC v. Radiation Technology. 519 Fed. Supp. 1266. (D.NJ 1981).

57. USAEC Order to Isomedix, Inc. re: Byproduct Material Licenses No.'s 29-15364-01 and 29-15364-02, June 14, 1974. USNRC Notice of Violation and letter to Isomedix, May 17, 1977. USNRC Notice of Violation and letter to Isomedix, September 4, 1979. Letter from Thomas T. Martin, USNRC, to Isomedix, Docket No. 30-19752, October 18, 1984.

58. NRC Inspection Report for Isomedix. Docket No. 30-08985, dated July 7, 1981.

59. Memo from James H. Joyner to Vandy L. Miller, February 1982.

# CHAPTER 6

# IS IRRADIATION NEEDED?

"a new technology that can produce benefits to consumers"
United States Health and Human Services Secretary
Otis R. Bowen, April 1986

"After all, industry does not need irradiated food."
Dr. Ari Brynjolfsson, in *Food Preservation by Irradiation*, 1978

IN THIS CHAPTER we will examine some of the arguments that have been put forward for why irradiation of food is needed. We will be seeking to discover where there is a real need so that we can reach a balanced view of the benefits and disadvantages.

## Shelf Life and Food Quality

The effects of irradiation on food are regarded as desirable because they increase the storage time, or "shelf life," of foods. Irradiation should not, however, be regarded as a panacea for all food preservation problems. Along with the desired effects, a number of highly undesirable ones are produced. Reducing some (but not all) of them may be possible through use of heat or of very low temperatures, removal of oxygen during irradiation, or use of some chemical additives. In these cases, irradiation becomes only a part of the preservation process. In many cases, refrigeration will still be needed throughout the storage life of the product, and irradiation will not replace it as a major method of preservation. For long-term storage, sealed packaging may be needed, as recontamination can occur at any time. Yet, such packaging may induce other food hazards to develop, as we saw in Chapter 3.

Food irradiation should not be seen as a technical solution to all food hygiene problems. Indeed, its introduction has led to concealment of contamination of food, and could lead to a lowering of food hygiene standards and an increased risk to public health.

The appearance, feel, texture, taste, and smell of food are the most immediate perceptions of food quality. Various foods respond to irradiation in different ways. Irradiation may inhibit the ripening of fruit. It also produces a softening of the tissues and leaves many fruits more susceptible to bruising.

Of 27 fruits and vegetables investigated, the process has been found beneficial for only eight (see Table 11). Clearly, we need to be very selective about the use of irradiation of fruit.

Potatoes may be slower to sprout if irradiated. Once they have been irradiated, the bruising and cuts that occur in harvesting are also slower to heal. For this reason, a delay after harvesting is recommended before irradiation. At the same time, irradiation also increases the

## Table 11: Response of 27 Fruits and Vegetables to Irradiation

| Fruit | Beneficial Effects | | | Not Beneficial | | |
|---|---|---|---|---|---|---|
| | (a) | (b) | (c) | (d) | (e) | (f) |
| Bananas | * | | | | | |
| Mangoes | * | | | | | |
| Papayas | * | * | | | | |
| Sweet cherries | | * | | | | |
| Apricots | | * | | | | |
| Tomatoes | | | * | | | |
| Strawberries | | | * | | | |
| Figs | | | * | | | |
| Pears | | | | * | | |
| Avocados/nectarines | | | | * | | |
| Lemons | | | | * | | |
| Peaches | | | | | * | |
| Grapefruit/pineapples | | | | | | * |
| Oranges/lychees | | | | | | * |
| Tangerines/honeydew/melon | | | | | | * |
| Cucumbers | | | | | | * |
| Summer squash | | | | | | * |
| Bell peppers | | | | | | * |
| Olives | | | | | | * |
| Plums | | | | | | * |
| Apples | | | | | | * |
| Table grapes | | | | | | * |
| Cantaloupes | | | | | | * |

| | |
|---|---|
| (a) delay in ripening | (d) damaged by radiation |
| (b) delay in aging | (e) accelerated ripening |
| (c) control of storage decay | (f) no positive benefit |
| (Source: Reference 3.) | |

susceptibility to subsequent fungus attack and rotting. Careful inspection and sorting must remove soil and any potatoes that are rotten or damaged; otherwise, the whole batch will quickly spoil. It may be that these factors, brought on by particularly adverse damp harvesting conditions, were reasons for the financial failure of the Canadian Potato Irradiation project in the mid-1960s.[1]

Onions, on the other hand, are best irradiated within 4 weeks of harvesting. Damaged or rotting onions also easily spoil the whole batch. Both onions and garlic show signs of internal browning after irradiation,[2] a factor that reduces their commercial value.

Milk and milk products do not irradiate well. Phrases such as "chalky," "scorched," "candle-like," or "burned wool" have been used to describe the flavor and smell of irradiated milk.[3]

Fats also suffer from irradiation. "Musty," "nutty," or "oily" have been used to describe the effects. Oils suffer even more. This is of particular importance in attempts to treat oily fish—mackerel, for example.[3]

Meat, one of the main foods for which high-dose treatments are being developed, develops what has been characterized as a "wet dog" smell.[3,4] Damage to the tissues of meat also causes excess bleeding, making it less attractive and, as we shall see, requiring the use of chemical additives to bind the liquid into the meat and so keep the weight up.

The exact nature of what has been called these "typical irradiation flavors" and odors has not yet been fully characterized. Perhaps even more significantly, the major culprits in terms of the foods' chemistry have not been fully identified. Clearly, little is fully understood about the massive and random rearrangement of the molecular structure of the proteins, fats, carbohydrates, enzymes, and residual chemicals in these foods.

Clearly, the claim that irradiation can extend shelf life of foods needs to be qualified. In some specific cases and under some fairly restrictive conditions, this may be true. Rather than giving a general clearance to the process as proposed by the Codex Alimentarius of the United Nations, the early United States procedure of permitting its use only for specific foods seems to be more realistic. It would have been better still if the appropriate conditions for each food had been regulated as well. As it is, the opportunity to establish specific

food-by-food controls is fast disappearing with the general clearance
of irradiation up to 100,000 rad (1 kGy).

## Pesticides and Insect Infestation

One of the strongest arguments that can be made for irradiation of
fruit is the need to control insect infestation, as growers in California
and Florida, fighting the Mediterranean fruit fly, will testify.

These states have resorted to various control measures in recent
years, including biological controls, such as releasing large numbers
of sterile male insects, and chemical controls. In California state
authorities considered it necessary to engage in aerial spraying of
the pesticide malathion onto residential communities in 1981. The
inability of these measures to eliminate the Medfly problem requires
quarantine measures and the fumigation of fruit before it goes out
of the state.

This approach is also needed for some fruit imports, e.g., mangoes
and papayas. Strict controls are maintained at all ports and airports
to prevent infestation from abroad. Other countries apply similar controls. A similar concern arises over infestation in spices and, to a
lesser extent, in wheat and other grains.

In each case, some workers are inevitably exposed to the chemical
pesticides used. The United States has recently banned some uses
of ethylene dibromide (EDB). The EEC will institute a complete
ban on its use by 1989. Other chemicals that are known or suspected
to be harmful are also being phased out.

Obviously, any safer alternative to the use of such chemical
treatments is to be welcomed. However, we do have to weigh the
concerns over worker safety in irradiation plants against the hazards
of pesticide use. The safety, wholesomeness, and controllability
issues outlined in the previous chapters also need to be weighed
against the benefits of removing pesticide residues from fruit and
other food.[5]

Alternatives to either chemical fumigants or irradiation include
oxygenless air, cold storage, or heat treatment to kill insect pests. Some
stored grain in Australia is treated with carbon dioxide gas ($CO_2$).
Provided the grain silo is properly sealed, its contents can generally
be stored for four months without infestation.[6]

The Hawaiian papaya industry suffered a severe shock when EDB was banned in 1984. The initial attempts to heat-treat the fruit to kill insect larvae resulted in hard lumpy papayas that would not ripen, threatening the industry's exports to the rest of the United States and Japan. It was initially thought that irradiation would be the only viable alternative. However, Japan does not permit the importation of irradiated fruit, and one papaya packing house ships 80% of its fruit to Japan. This has effectively killed any hope that irradiation will be adopted as the alternative. By 1985, acceptable "double dip" and steam vapor heat treatments had been developed, and by 1986 five of the six major packing plants were using these methods. Several of the packing companies have stated they will not use irradiation. An irradiation plant would be barely economically viable, even if all the state's papayas intended for shipping to the mainland United States were treated in this way. To achieve this level of irradiation would require abandoning the heat-dipping technology in which many companies have already invested.[7]

Thus, in the case of papayas, we see that pressures to find alternatives to both chemical fumigants and irradiation have led to other technological advances. Even though there is now no technological need and certainly no commercial incentive to build an irradiation facility, the DOE has offered the state one of the six demonstration irradiation plants it is proposing to help build and pay for.

Denmark has recently developed a protein coating that will permit heat treatment of many spices. In other cases, alternatives to hazardous chemicals may be more difficult to find. If, in the final analysis, irradiation is found to be safer and more cost-effective than any of the alternatives, we should certainly consider its use on a case-by-case basis for specific fruits, spices, and other foods. In these cases, its introduction should be linked to bans on the other, more harmful, chemical processes so that they are phased out. Failure to link the introduction of irradiation to such bans will lead to a situation where we are likely to have the disadvantages of not one or the other technology, but both.

## Irradiation and Additives

In Britain, one of the major initial selling points in favor of food irradiation has been the claim that it will reduce the need for harmful chemical additives in food.[8,9,10,11,12,13]

There is a very real and well-founded public concern about the extent to which foods are being adulterated with chemicals. Processed foods rely on additives not merely for preservative effects but for flavors, colors, and bulk fillers as well. In addition to the concern about pesticide residues in food and the harmful effects they have on agricultural and other workers,[5] we are also concerned about the effect of food additives on both consumers and workers.[14]

It is particularly alarming to find that far from eliminating additive use, the process of irradiation will itself require the use of several additives in order to control some of the undesirable effects of irradiation.[3] Table 12 lists some of the additives that are claimed to be eliminated or reduced by irradiation and those proposed for use with irradiation.

The use of such additives is not to be restricted to the high-dose applications where the obnoxious radiation flavors become pronounced, but are also proposed for low-dose uses to prevent discoloration and other undesirable effects such as bleeding and breakdown of fats in meat. To control these effects, the following steps for preservation treatment of meat are proposed:

1. Cut into portions.
2. Dip in a dilute solution of sodium tripolyphosphate* (or other condensed phosphate).
3. Filmwrap.
4. Vacuum pack film-wrapped portions in a bulk container.
5. Refrigerate at 0 to 5 °C.
6. Irradiate with a dose of 1 to 2 kGy.
7. Ship and store at 0 to 5 °C.
8. Remove from container for display no more than one-half hour before display.
9. Refrigerate display at 0 to 5 °C.
10. Sell within 3 days.

In this way, it is proposed to extend the shelf life of retail cuts of meat to 21 days.[3]

---

*Sodium tripolyphosphate is a chemical used for cleaning grime off walls (it cuts grease). It is also irritating to the skin and is used as a purgative as well as in food preservation.[15]

## Table 12: Irradiation and Additives

| Some hazardous additives which it is claimed irradiation might replace. | | Some additives which might be needed to reduce undesirable effects of radiation. | |
|---|---|---|---|
| *E251 Sodium nitrite | m,c | *E251 Sodium nitrite | m,c |
| *F230 Diphenyl | c, | *E230 Diphenyl | c, |
| E220 Sulphur dioxide | c, | E221 Sodium sulphite | i, |
| E210 Benzoic acid | a,i, | E300 Ascorbic acid | |
| Propylene glycol | c, | E321 B.H.T. | c, |
| 925 Chlorine | i, | E320 B.H.A. | c, |
| E926 Chlorine dioxide | i, | 371 Nicotinic acid | i,a |
| E281 Sodium propionate | a, | 924 Potassium bromate | i, |
| E236 Formic acid (banned in UK) | i, | Sodium tripoly-phosphate (TPP) | i, |
| Ethylene oxide | c,i,m,t, | Sodium chloride (salt) | |
| Methyl bromide | i, | Glutathione (for vitamin $B_1$) | |
| Ethylene dibromide | i,c, | Niacin (for vitamin $B_6$) | |
| Propylene oxide | i, | Sodium ascorbate (for vitamin C) | |
| Hydrogen peroxide | i, | | |

Key:
i = irritant, c = carcinogen (known or suspected cancer causing agent in animals and/or humans), m = mutagen (capable of causing mutations), t = teratogen (capable of causing damage to developing fetus), a = capable of causing allergic reactions.
(Source: Reference 3. Hazards information; References 14, 34.)

Since some enzymes are destroyed by irradiation, whereas others increase their activity, it is proposed to treat slaughter animals with Adrenalin if the meat is to be irradiated. This is to reduce the activity of the enzymes that cause fermentation, which dissolves the proteins in meat.[16]

Some of the additives in Table 12 are vitamin supplements designed to make good the sometimes severe nutrient losses discussed in Chapter 4. Perhaps, in view of the concerns raised over such losses, there is a case for requiring the use of vitamins as additives to make good the losses in irradiated foods. Even so, there is evidence that there are differences between vitamins added to irradiated foods and those added to foods not irradiated.[6]

Approval of irradiation, if it is given, should be linked to bans and other restrictions on the use of chemical additives that are currently used as preservatives, and to legislation designed to maintain the nutritional quality of irradiated foods, by vitamin supplementation if necessary. Unless this is done, we will be adding to the range of hazards—not, as those in favor of irradiation claim, reducing the current adulteration of foods.

## Food Poisoning

National and international agencies have recently placed considerable emphasis on the need for irradiation to reduce the level of food poisoning. The Food Irradiation newsletter published by the FAO/IAEA states, "no technology is available to produce raw foods of animal origin, particularly poultry and pork, in which the absence of certain pathogenic microorganisms such as *Salmonella, Campylobacter, Toxoplasma,* and *Trichinella* can be guaranteed. These foods pose a serious threat to public health."[17]

The scale of the problem is not in dispute. There is no doubt that food poisoning is a major cause of ill health, not only in the United States, where some 40,000 cases are estimated to occur each year,[18] but in many other countries also. Rather, the question is, how strong is the case for irradiation as the solution?

Let us consider *Salmonella* in chicken. Most fresh, chilled, and frozen chicken carcasses today contain some *Salmonella.* The bacteria are inactivated by freezing, and their growth is considerably retarded if they are refrigerated below 41°F (5°C). They start growing rapidly again at room temperatures but can be killed completely if the food is properly cooked. Leaving cooked food around the kitchen, particularly if it comes into contact with surfaces and utensils (or unwashed hands) that have been in contact with the raw meat, will result in recontamination and further rapid multiplication of the bacteria.

Proper cooking and good kitchen hygiene are 100% effective in protecting people from *Salmonella.* In many cases, however, a breakdown in food hygiene can lead to outbreaks of food poisoning. These are usually mild in the home but can be more serious in restaurants and institutions, where food is often kept warm longer.

To totally eliminate this problem will be difficult whatever route we take. We could irradiate all chicken. We would probably need to irradiate all other meats as well. Even then, recontamination could still occur. Partial use of irradiation might reduce the scale of the problem. Equally, it might, unless accompanied by a food hygiene education program that warned of the danger, lead to a false sense of security, a lowering of hygiene standards, and more food poisoning outbreaks.

Even if we could get the benefits of irradiation without the risks of food poisoning, is this the best way to deal with the problem of bacterial contamination of food?

*Salmonella* is not an inevitable contaminant in the meat of chickens. It is, however, endemic in chicken feed and so contaminates the bowel of most chickens. It is spread to the meat if the gut is burst during processing. At this stage, good food hygiene would require that the process wash the bird and, if it is being done manually, that the process worker wash his or her hands. Failure to do so will spread *Salmonella*-contaminated feces to every other bird on the processing line.

We could deal with this by building an irradiator at the end of every chicken processing line, but in doing so we would be legitimizing poor food hygiene and handling practices. We do not think it would help promote chicken sales if the consumer was told that a bird had been irradiated to conceal the fact that it had been contaminated with chicken feces. Would it not be better to tackle the problem at its source—by eliminating the *Salmonella* in the feed, and by rigorous food hygiene in processing plants?

In Britain, this has been done in some well-monitored cases. Irradiation of animal feed has been legal for some years now. Salmonella contamination of the flock at the Cambridgeshire poultry research station was eliminated by irradiating the feed. Local health officials have testified to eliminating salmonella problems in U.K. processing plants by working closely with the staff on improving hygiene.[19]

A Canadian study lists benefit/cost comparisons for eleven *Salmonella* control options. Public education, use of chlorinated chill water in packing houses, adequate cleaning, disinfestation of poultry crates in transport and the poultry processing industry generally are all seen as five to eight times more effective than irradiation, with other disinfection and feed sterilization techniques being almost as effective.[20] What evidence is there that these approaches have been tried and found not to work in the United States?

As we discussed in Chapter 3, elimination of *Salmonella* by irradiation could leave chicken more vulnerable to growth of *C. botulinum*, without the warning smell that tells people the meat has spoiled. Whatever method we use to tackle the problem of food poisoning, it will not eliminate the need for kitchen hygiene and thorough cooking, nor the need to prevent people having a false sense of security: meat can become recontaminated at any time.

In the case of fish, it has been found that high-pressure washing of the fish can extend the normal shelf life from the current 4 to 6 days to about 11 to 17 days. Use of sanitized water in the wash could further reduce the bacterial load and extend its life even more. The cost would be a few cents per fish. A shelf life of over 16 days for "fresh" fish is not currently seen as valuable by the fish industry. Beyond this period, freezing already provides adequate storage capability.

## Trichinosis in Pork

The other area of current concern in the United States is the need to eliminate the *Trichinella* parasite found in pork. There are currently only 45 to 70 cases a year.[18] Nevertheless, at the request of irradiation companies, the FDA has recently approved the use of irradiation to render sterile the trichina larvae in pork to prevent them from reproducing inside the bodies of people who eat the contaminated meat.

It is very hard to see any objective justification for this. The few cases of trichinae contamination that have been found are due to inspection failure in the system administered by the USDA. Trichinae are effectively killed by thorough cooking anyway, so the few cases of trichinosis that occur are again due to poor kitchen practice. Pork has traditionally had a reputation as a meat requiring care in cooking. Perhaps it is this image that pork producers are trying to change by use of irradiation, rather than any specific problem with trichinae. If so, we run the risks already identified of creating a false sense of security, as the doses allowed so far will not be sufficient to deactivate other food hazards. If it results in fewer inspections and hence more contaminated carcasses, we feel sure that pork sales will not be helped. Consumers need to realize that the trichina larvae will not be killed but only rendered incapable of breeding inside their bodies. Better inspection would be better, cheaper, and safer than irradiation.

The argument for irradiation as a necessity for trichina elimination is in fact a weak one. Inexpensive testing options exist that could identify infected hogs at the slaugherhouse, and the source could then be traced and eliminated. We suspect irradiation is being used more as a way of getting a toe in the door—as a forerunner for clearance of much higher doses of radiation for pork and other meats—than because of any specific need to deal with a health problem.

## Food Wastage

> Development agencies tell us that one billion people (one out of every five of us) go to bed hungry every night and that 35,000 people die daily from hunger and hunger related causes. Radioisotopes and radiation used in food and agriculture are helping reduce these terrible figures.
>
> Isotopes in Day to Day Life, IAEA June 1984

Perhaps the strongest argument put forward for irradiation is the need to prevent some of the wastage of food that occurs, particularly in third world countries that may have difficulty feeding their own population and that may be dependent on food aid as a result.

For farmers in the developed Western countries, currently facing large food surpluses, falling prices, and needing government support to encourage them to grow less, the idea of saving more food may not seem to be so important. Both the United States and the EEC have massive surpluses, and the problem is rather what to do with them, how to store them, and how to pay for them. The Soviet Union does use irradiation for treating stored grain. Its grain irradiation facility at Odessa, of 400,000 tons a year, dwarfs the total volume of irradiated food in all other countries. The United States, on the other hand, has had permits for grain irradiation since 1963, and to date there is no significant use of the technology. Recently, Radiant Energy, Inc., in Lynchburg,

Virginia, has confirmed that it has been irradiating some wheat for use in bread products.[21]

We have seen no evidence from American farmers that there is a need for irradiation to reduce food wastage. Similarly, in Europe, the mountains of food are an embarrassment for farmers and politicians of all EEC countries. In Britain, the regional Farmers Unions and the farming press have come out vigorously against irradiation on the grounds of there being no need for it, and for health reasons.[22]

How real is the concern for the third world? In many of these countries, the primary need is for improved harvesting and transportation systems that would enable poor farmers to get their produce to market, and for dry storage facilities to protect the storable produce from damp and humid conditions. If dry storage were provided, then some methods of temperature control would be the next step. It is here that irradiation is offered as an alternative. It is claimed that the energy costs of irradiation would be less than those of cool storage and refrigeration. There is little evidence to support this. As we have seen throughout this book, irradiation rarely provides an alternative to other food preservation technologies. Often it can be used with refrigeration, but rarely replaces it. The energy equation is by no means as simple as it would appear. Certainly, if the West were to make available the radioactive isotopes to these poorer countries, or they were to obtain them from the wastes from their own nuclear programs, it might be economically viable. However, the total costs of the systems, including all the money and energy needed to run the competing systems, are unlikely to show clear advantages for irradiation. At a practical level, if we really want to help the third world countries in their problems, there are many things we can and should do before we even suggest that they buy into irradiation technology.

Rather than a dream that irradiation will solve the problems of the world's food supply, we have a nightmare that the food surpluses of the developed world will be stored longer by use of irradiation, and these nutritionally depleted foods will then be off-loaded onto the third world—with insult added to injury as we call it "aid." In return, the wealthier sections of their own farming communities will be able to export more of the exotic produce for consumption in the rich countries of the world. The gap between those who have and those who starve is not likely to be narrowed—unless, that is, there are major social and political changes within those countries and between us and them. We do not hear any talk of such changes taking place alongside and as part of the process of providing appropriate technical aid.

## The Economics of Food Irradiation

Consumers want quality food at a price they can afford. The quality of irradiated foods is, as we have seen, questionable, either because of the invisible damage done by irradiation or because lower-quality foods are those more likely to be irradiated and marketed along with the high-quality fresh product. This lower-quality food may even marginally undercut the price of the high-quality product while looking as good or better.

The costs of food irradiation are likely to depend on a variety of factors, including capital costs of irradiation plants, costs of radiation sources, types and quantities of foods to be irradiated, transport costs, seasonality of food, the market image of irradiated foods, and competition from other processes. The 1981 report of the FAO/IAEA/WHO called for investigation of the economic prospects for food irradiation,[23] and an international IAEA symposium raised many unanswered questions regarding economics.[24]

Some people argue that the markeplace will sort out all these problems. If the price is right, the consumer will buy irradiated foods. If not, then irradiation won't happen. Reality is more complex than this simple grocery-store view of national economics.

As well as the effect on prices to the consumer, a full study of the economics of food irradiation should consider the impact the technology would have on the whole food industry, on employment within the industry, and on patterns of marketing and consumption. Just as hidden subsidies can make a process appear financially beneficial, many hidden social costs could indicate that it is, after all, undesirable. Such a study would help in assessing claims made about the economic benefits of food irradiation.

## Costs of Irradiation Plant

There are currently about 70 food irradiation plants operating, planned, or under construction world-wide. They vary from portable field units to large-scale, multipurpose irradiation plants. There are, in addition, several facilities dealing in sterilization of medical products, some of which could become involved in food irradiation.

In the United States there are about 60 facilities that are currently licensed to irradiate medical supplies. Of these, 17 are licensed to irradiate food[21,25] (see Appendix 1).

The DOE proposes to build a further six plants and has obtained appropriations of $10 million from the United States government for this in fiscal years 1986 and 1987. Obviously, the costs of building such plants vary widely. A large-scale production facility based on an American design was priced at $2 million in 1984. James Deitch, formerly with the Department of Commerce, estimated back in 1982 that capital costs for a 3 million curie cobalt 60 source plant would then have been $1.1 million.[26] A recently commissioned facility for Isotron Ltd. in Britain cost $4.5 million.[27]

The USDA has suggested plant costs ranging from $1 million to $11.2 million.[24] The bigger the plant, the greater the economies of scale. However, the USDA concluded that the economic cost/benefit equation has not yet been determined, as actual costs will be unclear until variable factors such as seasonal use, transportation, and consumer acceptability are assessed.

A major running cost in an irradiation plant is the radioactive source. The amount of radioactive source material will depend on the type of food (and hence the dose required) and the amount to be processed. At current market prices, a 1 million curie source of cobalt needed for a large facility would initially cost about $1.1 million with replacement costs of about $150,000 per year.[28]

On the other hand, if you have something that no one wants, you can usually justify giving it away. The costs of cobalt 60 from Canada, where it is produced by neutron bombardment of cobalt 59 in a Candu Reactor, is about $1.10 per curie (Ci), whereas the DOE is offering to lease cesium 137 at 10.0 cents per Ci.[29] Why? The simple fact is that the cesium is currently part of that rather awkward problem—nuclear waste—which no one quite knows what to do with, and which most communities, and the vast majority of state governments, want to keep outside their borders.

There are currently no reliable estimates of the cost of extracting the cesium, which is one of the more active and moderately long-lived isotopes produced in spent fuel in nuclear reactors. The available supplies have come from reprocessing of the fuel used in weapons reactors where plutonium is produced for the nuclear bombs. There is currently no reprocessing of spent fuel from commercial reactors in the United States.

The alternative to either cobalt 60 or cesium 137 gamma ray sources is to use either x-rays or electrons. Both the initial capital investment and the annual running costs would be considerably less than for either a cobalt 60 or cesium 137 gamma ray source plant. In addition, the higher energy of the x-rays would permit the plant to process more food in the same time, and achieve a smaller difference between the maximum and minimum doses to the food package.[30]

On the basis of annual running costs, and even allowing for the DOE subsidy that offers cesium 137 at a tenth of the price of cobalt 60, it has been estimated that the cost per ton of food from an x-ray plant is three-fourths the cost of irradiating food in a cesium 137 plant and half that of a cobalt 60 plant—all plants of similar size and initial building costs.[30]

The use of x-ray facilities also lends itself more readily to small-scale field use, and thereby reduces some of the transport costs that are a significant part of the add-on costs for irradiation of food at a large central facility. Given these projections, one has to wonder why the gamma ray sources are being so heavily promoted and subsidized at this time.

In Britain, there are some 10 irradiation facilities currently handling medical supplies or animal feed. Of these, four, all owned by Isotron Ltd., could handle food irradiation if and when the British government permits the process. With costs on this scale, and with a virtual monopoly on the current British facilities, it is only natural to find considerable pressure from Isotron for removal of the current ban in the United Kingdom. We find similar pressures in the United States from leading spokespersons for irradiation companies such as Radiation Technology and Isomedix. In Britain, Frank Ley, a director of Isotron, was an advisor to the government's advisory committee on irradiated foods. Sir Arnold Burgen, the chairman of the committee, is a part-time director of Amersham International, Britain's leading isotope manufacturer.

Until now, the major source of radioactive cobalt 60 for the British plants has been Canada. Cobalt 60 may soon be produced in large quantities in Britain as radioactive wastes if permission to build the American-style pressurized water reactor (PWR) is granted. Cobalt 60 is produced in the steam generators and is the major radioactive component of the "crud" that has to be removed from them periodically during operation. In the meantime, the alternative isotope, cesium 137, exists in large quantities as waste from the Sellafield (formerly Windscale) reprocessing plant.[31,32]

France is the other country involved in commercial reprocessing of reactor fuel from several European countries.

The economics of food irradiation are thus very closely bound up with the costs of energy (in the case of x-ray units) and with the costs of cesium 137 and cobalt 60. These latter costs could come down significantly if cheap radioactive cobalt or cesium sources are provided as a way of dealing with the problem of nuclear wastes. Even so, the initial costs are high, and there will be considerable pressure to utilize the facilities to the full.

Either way, the costs will be passed on to the consumer. With bulk costs of about $3 to $6 per ton for food receiving the maximum dose in the United States, we can expect irradiation to add a few cents to many food items, provided that the transportation costs can be kept down and the plants operate to full capacity all the time. These costs may be optimistic. The Italian chapter of the International Organization of Consumer Unions has calculated that spread over a five-year period, the true cost of a proposed food irradiation plant would add $144 to the cost per ton of potatoes.[33]

The other major factor in the economic equation is the initial capital outlay to set up irradiation facilities. There just do not appear to be overwhelming economic advantages for the process that would justify such economic risks, especially as consumer reaction to irradiated food is uncertain and may be hostile. If the government is to enter into this field by building demonstration plants, we would expect that they at least choose the type of facility that offers the best economic prospects. The evidence to date suggests that even with the subsidized costs for cesium 137 from the DOE, neither the cesium nor cobalt gamma ray facilities meets this economic criterion. Why, then, is the cesium 137 option being promoted?

## Is Food Irradiation Necessary?

What is emerging is a picture of a process that, far from providing a solution to problems of food preservation, would be only one more step in a variety of food processing techniques: heating, refrigeration, use of chemical additives, reduction of oxygen and moisture, packaging, and hygienic handling. Irradiation actually adds to the complexity of food processing because it creates undesirable changes in the food. Many of the other techniques are necessary to reduce this radiation damage. It is perhaps worth asking the fundamental question whether irradiation is necessary at all.

The answer to this is by no means clear-cut. In the area of low doses there might be a justification for irradiation, but even here the overall benefits are by no means obvious. As we have seen, many fruits do not irradiate well; however, irradiation may produce less damage to the food (and be less harmful to the health of workers) than some chemical fumigation treatments for controlling insect infestations. This can be important where quarantine arrangements exist (e.g., to control the Mediterranean fruit fly). There are, however, no studies that provide a scientific basis for comparing the risks of the alternative processes. Other uses appear to have more to do with the ability of the food industry to stockpile or to deliver an apparently acceptable product for sale when long-distance shipments are involved. The benefits to the consumer in this area appear to be marginal, particularly when the effects on wholesomeness and nutritional value are considered.

Irradiation of grains to control infestation may also require control of atmosphere and temperature. Packaging is needed to control reinfestation. Under these circumstances, it is hard to see that there will be clear-cut economic benefits that could not be derived from the other techniques alone. By far the greatest food losses occur in the warm, moist, and less well-developed countries, which lack the capital to invest in such storage technology. Food irradiation, with its very high capital costs and complex technology rooted in the nuclear industry, would seem to be the least preferable of a series of measures that should be undertaken to improve the situation in these countries. To propose it seriously as the solution would inevitably mean that the food reserves of these countries would come even more under the control of multinational agribusiness than they already are. But then, that may be precisely why it is being proposed.

In the medium-dose range, which will soon come up for consideration in the United States and is already used in some other countries, the possibilities of detrimental effects outweighing benefits becomes even greater. The major use in this area is to reduce the number of microorganisms that cause food spoilage and require food processing, particularly in meats. Reduction, not elimination, is the goal. In the course of reducing *Salmonella* risks, we have seen the possibility of creating other more serious health hazards, the very real dangers of abuse of the technology to conceal serious contamination, and the possibility of a lowering of food hygiene standards.

Again, irradiation does not eliminate the need for refrigeration, packaging, and good food hygiene. Food irradiation researcher W. M. Urbain has questioned whether its use is warranted.

> The doses involved . . . exceed the threshold doses for irradiated flavor development in meats if done above 0 degrees C. Irradiation at sub freezing temperatures would overcome this. However, in view of the rather large costs that would be involved in such processing, including; freezing, irradiation and thawing, it seems unlikely that a meat processor would undertake it voluntarily. While government regulations could impose radicidation [irradiation], the risk benefit balance for the consumer would need to be considered. In terms of the costs to the consumer, it appears to this author, to be an unwarranted application of irradiation.[35]

Urbain goes on to point out that most parasites are inactivated by the freezing temperatures needed to prevent off flavors in irradiated meats anyway. Further irradiation for this purpose seems to be unnecessary.

If radicidation (at medium doses) to reduce the level of microorganisms is of marginal benefit, radappertization (at high doses) is likely to be even less so. The undesirable effects in terms of food odor, creation of radiolytic chemicals, and changes in microbiological balances will be more pronounced. Refrigeration to very low temperatures ($-20$ to $-80\,^{\circ}$C), use of additives, packaging to eliminate oxygen and prevent recontamination, and so on will all be essential to reduce these effects. While this will allow food to be stored for long periods, the existing methods are already able to do this to a large extent. Since these will still be needed, it is unclear where the advantage lies.

Irradiation can be used to reduce the heat required for sterilization just as heat can be used to reduce the amount of radiation needed. It may be that some combination of heat and irradiation treatment could overcome some of the disadvantages of irradiation, though the overall balance of risks and benefits is far from clear.

A few high-technology applications are always cited as proving the need for irradiation, such as diets for astronauts and for medical patients undergoing transplant surgery. In Britain, where irradiation for sterile medical diets is already recognized and permitted, at least one major hospital has discontinued its use, finding it "of little benefit". It is nice to be able to experiment with "space age" food techniques, but the decision to permit wholesale irradiation at these high doses should surely follow clear evidence of need, particularly as the technology introduces so many distinct problems and hazards.

In short, it is hard to see where there are overriding benefits from food irradiation that would justify the pressures we have experienced for the rapid introduction of food irradiation at this time. One has to ask, is there something else, some hidden agenda that would account for this pressure, this haste to gain approval for irradiation, and for the way in which concerns about safety, wholesomeness, and controllability have been given short shrift.

REFERENCES

1. L. Pim. *Gamma Irradiation as a Means of Food Preservation in Canada.* Pollution Probe Foundation, Toronto, 1983.
2. P. S. Elias and A. J. Cohen. *Recent Advances in Food Irradiation.* Amsterdam and New York: Elsevier Biomedical Press, 1983.
3. Edward S. Josephson and Martin S. Peterson, eds. *Preservation of Food by Ionizing Radiation* (3 vols.). Florida: CRC Press, Vol. 1 1982, Vols. 2 & 3 1983.
4. M. D. Rankin, ed., in *Food Industries Manual,* 21st edition. Glasgow: Leonard Hill/Blackie, 1984.
5. Pete Snell. *Pesticide Residues and Food—A Case for Real Control.* London Food Commission, London, 1986.

6. Rosanna Mentzer Morrison and Tanya Roberts. *Food Irradiation: New Perspectives on a Controversial Technology—A Review of Technical, Public Health and Economic Considerations.* Report prepared for the Office of Technology Assessment, Congress of the United States, by the Economic Research Service of the US Department of Argriculture, Washington, DC, December 1985.

7. Kathy Dorn. *Briefing on the Hawaiian Papaya Industry and Irradiation.* East Hawaii Chapter, NCSFI, August 1986.

8. Robert Millar. *Coming Soon . . . Atom Rays That Keep Food Fresh. Daily Express* (London), 4 February 1985.

9. Sue Thomas. Irradiated Food: The Facts and Fears. *Woman Magazine* (London), 16 March 1985.

10. Carmen Konopka. Novel Food Storage Techniques. *Caterer and Hotelkeeper* (Sutton, England), 2 May 1985.

11. Gamma is Good for You. *The Economist* (London), 22 January 1985.

12. Denise Winn. Can You Live with Long Life Food. *Cosmopolitan,* July 1985.

13. Janette Marshall. Food That Doesn't Go Off. *Here's Health* (West Byfleet, England), August 1985.

14. Melanie Miller. *Danger! Additives at Work.* London Food Commission, London, 1985.

15. M. Windholz, ed. *The Merck Index: An Encyclopedia of Chemicals and Drugs* (9th ed.). Rahway, New Jersey: Merck & Co., 1976.

16. Judith A. DeCava. Facts About Food Irradiation. *Journal of the National Academy of Research Biochemists,* 652, July 1986.

17. Joint FAO/IAEA Division of Isotope and Radiation Applications of Atomic Energy for Food and Agricultural Development. *Food Irradiation Newsletter,* Vol. 10, No 2, IAEA, Vienna, November 1986.

18. Figures from US Center for Disease Control, Atlanta, Georgia.

19. Panel discussion during one-day seminar: Food Irradiation—Assessing the Risks and Benefits. Institution of Environmental Health Officers, London, January 22, 1987.

20. Leo Curtin. Economic Study of Salmonella Poisoning and Control Measures in Canada. Food Markets Analysis Division, Marketing and Economics Branch, Agriculture, Ottawa, Canada, August 1984.

21. *Food Irradiation Response Newsletter.* December 1986/January 1987, Santa Cruz, California.

22. Tony Webb and Tim Lang. *Food Irradiation: The Facts.* London: Thorsons, 1987.

23. World Health Organization. *Wholesomeness of Irradiated Food.* Report of Joint FAO/IAEA/WHO Expert Committee. WHO Technical Report Series No. 659, Geneva, 1981.

24. IAEA. *Food Irradiation Processing.* Proceedings of a Symposium held in March 1985, IAEA, Vienna, September 1985.

25. Nuclear Regulatory Commission. Active NRC Licenses—Irradiators other >10,000 curies, September 1986. NRC In-house Irradiation Facilities, September 1986.

26. James Deitch. Economics of Food Irradiation. 17 CRC. Critical Review in Food Science and Nutrition, 17, 307, 1982.

27. Terry Garrett. Isotron Profits Expected to Exceed £1 Million Mark. *Financial Times* (London), 1 July 1985.

28. *Preliminary Assessment Data for an Irradiation Service Facility.* Simon Food Engineering Ltd, Stockport, UK, 1984.

29. HEI telephone call to Sylvia Wolfeat, DOE Oak Ridge Laboratory, February 8, 1987: CS 137 will be leased at 10¢ per curie.

30. M. G. Lagunas-Solar and S. M. Matthews. Comparative Economic Factors on the Use of Radionuclide or Electrical Sources for Food Processing with Ionizing Radiation. *Radiation Physics and Chemistry,* Vol. 25, Nos 1-3, 1985.

31. British Nuclear Fuels Evidence, Windscale Inquiry, UK, 1977.

32. CEGB evidence to Sizewell Inquiry, UK, 1983.

33. Andrea Gaifami. *Food Irradiation and Madame Curie's Cuisine.* Quaderni di Controinformazione alimentare. Milan, Italy, Spring 1986.

34. N. H. Proctor and J. P. Hughes. *Chemical Hazards in the Workplace.* Philadelphia: Lippincott, 1978.

35. W. M. Urbain. In: Edward S. Josephson and Martin S. Peterson, eds. *Preservation of Food by Ionizing Radiation,* Vol. 3. Florida: CRC Press, 1983.

# CHAPTER 7

# WHO WANTS IT?

## A Strategy for Acceptance?

The following represents part of the marketing plan for getting us, or more particularly our governments, to accept and persuade us to use irradiated foods.[1]

To achieve the approval, acceptance and usage of food irradiation on a world-wide basis:
1. Encourage appropriate government organizations to approve/ regulate and endorse food irradiation.
2. Encourage appropriate nongovernment organizations to approve and accept food irradiation.
3. Convince the food industry as a whole to accept and use the food irradiation process.
4. Convince consumers to buy and eat irradiated food.

To convince our governments to accept the technology the plan proposes:
1. Identifying key decision makers, "organizationally and personally."
2. Providing these decision makers with "complete information packages about food irradiation; its history, its safety, its efficacy, and consumer benefits."
3. Approaching WHO "to declare food irradiation a significant method of reducing food-borne diseases" and FAO "to endorse the importance of irradiation in post-harvest pest control and loss reduction."
4. Requesting the UN committee on Trade Aid and Development, and the General Agreement on Tariffs and Trade to "formally declare that food irradiation can exercise a positive impact on international trade."

5. Contacting "key decision makers on a personal basis to gain approval of food irradiation."
6. Undertaking "an indepth economic study of production processing and consumer reaction."
7. Using personal contacts to "persuade food handling unions to support food irradiation as a residue-free process and invite union representatives to cooperate with the lead organizations" (i.e., coalitions for food irradiation) in each country.
8. Approaching "food industry, irradiation processors, etc., to raise funds and promote food irradiation."
9. Engaging "a public relations company and/or communication consultancy to motivate food handling unions, consumer organizations and print media to recognize the benefits and accept the application of food irradiation." (IAEA/FAO International Consultative Group, 1986).

Many of these recommendations also appear in the joint FAO/IAEA Food Irradiation Newsletter.[2] The IAEA proposes the following:

- The WHO should publish a report on the benefits of irradiation with a view to requesting that national authorities adopt food irradiation as a method to control food-borne infection.
- Seminars/symposia on the contribution of irradiation to food safety should be convened by the FAO/IAEA and WHO in different regions.
- Medical groups (such as national institutes of health, centers for communicable diseases, national medical associations,) and national food trade associations should be invited to evaluate the application of irradiation to control food-borne infection and to publicize the outcome of these evaluations.
- The WHO should be invited to publish a brochure on the risk versus benefit of irradiation with emphasis on the public health implication, and give it to national medical associations for distribution among their members.
- National authorities should be encouraged to survey the incidence of food-borne illness and calculate the costs in lost wages and productivity.

- Mass media should be involved in informing the public of the benefit of irradiation.
- Special programs to promote its use in Latin America should:

Compare this technology with those already in existence and in use for food preservation, with a view to demonstrating its advantages.

Stress the harmlessness of the process.

Emphasize the effectiveness and versatility of the practical applications of this technology.

Stress that this preservation technology is a physical process and not a food additive.

Accept the "proven safe dose level of 10 kGy."

Promote the general use of the logo (Radura label) designed by The Netherlands as a symbol for irradiated commodities.

The newsletter concludes, "Each participant in this workshop on food irradiation will take appropriate measures with a view to the adoption of legislation governing food irradiation, following (the UN) Codex Alimentarius standards, in his respective country."[2]

Clearly, some very heavy international lobbying is going on to gain acceptance and approval for food irradiation, particularly in third world countries.

As we have seen, the experts appear to be foreclosing the debate on safety and wholesomeness. There has been little consideration of how the technology is to be controlled, and it is by no means clear that it is actually needed or that the benefits cannot be obtained by other methods with less risk to public health. Yet, there are considerable pressures for wholesale and widespread introduction of the process. Why? Who wants it? Who stands to benefit, and what do they stand to gain from the rapid introduction of food irradiation at this time?

## The Food Industry?

The food industry is the largest in the United States in terms of shipments and the third largest in terms of contribution to gross national product (GNP). Some 66% of all the food produced by 2.5 million farmers is processed by only 20,000 manufacturing companies before being sold through half a million distributing companies. Many of the manufacturers are small. Ninety-six percent have fewer than

100 employees. However, the 700 companies who employ more than 100 people have about 80% of the business. In terms of any particular food, the business can be dominated by even fewer firms. In most cases, fewer than 20 firms will control about 90% of a specific food market. These firms are both large and powerful. While profits in farming have been steadily declining, those in manufacturing have risen. There have also been mergers and takeovers, so that the whole processing industry is dominated by fewer and fewer large corporations, each producing a wide range of food products. The 20 largest corporations now control nearly 30% of the food market as a whole.[3]

In the food distribution sector we find a similar picture. There are three main channels through which we buy our food: the large retail chains, which increasingly market their own brand or "generic" brand products; the small independent stores, many of which have entered into cooperative buying arrangements to get better deals from the food manufacturers; and the restaurant and institutional food service trade, which has about 15% of the total food sales in the United States. Approximately 50% of food in the retail stores reaches us through only 40 companies. The 20 largest grocery chains have 37% of the total volume of food sales. They buy direct from manufacturers. The 20 largest wholesalers dominate the remainder of the trade, which goes through the independent grocers.[3]

The concentration of supermarket power is even more dramatic in particular cities. In any one city, the four largest retailers will frequently control 60% or more of all food sales. A small manufacturer finds it very hard to market a food product in Washington, D.C., if Safeway or Giant refuses to put it on the shelves, or similarly in Denver if it is rejected by King Soopers (Kroger) and Safeway. The retailers can also dictate the price, quality, packaging, labeling, and formula to be used in the processed foods that the manufacturers supply. In some cases, the retailers are also manufacturers. The largest eight supermarket chains supply 9% of their sales from foods they manufacture themselves. This market power may not always be used against the large manufacturers, but it is often used against smaller food processors, who have little choice but to accept the terms the supermarkets dictate.

By contrast, the import/export trade accounts for only 1% of the domestic market.[3] Even so, this is over 10% of the total world trade in food, second only to that of the EEC, which has 17% of the total. As we noted earlier, international trade is becoming increasingly important in providing exotic and out-of-season foods from other countries.

Advertising plays an increasingly important role in the food market. Again, this is dominated by the large corporations, where the 100 largest do 92% of all advertising and 99.9% of all network television food ads.[3]

Even this picture understates the full extent of concentration of market power. The largest firms are linked to each other in a network of overlapping stockholders, directors, financial ties, and other business contacts.[3]

The United States is not alone. A similar concentration of power exists in other developed countries. In Britain, for example, all farmland is owned by about 2% of the population. In food manufacturing, there are about 5,000 firms but the ten largest companies account for one-third of all sales. Approximately two-thirds of the trade in some food manufacturing sectors, such as oils, fats, biscuits, and bread, is controlled by the top 10 companies. In food retailing, the top nine companies control over half of the market. The number of retail outlets nearly halved between 1974 and 1983. Even in catering—a sector famous for its small businesses—the top 10 companies control nearly 60% of the contract catering market.[4]

Many consumers believe that retailers and manufacturers of food all think alike. They don't. Ever since the 1970s, they have been fighting an often bitter battle between themselves over prices and profit margins. Retailers currently hold the sway. With so few retailers dominating the consumer market in any city, what manufacturer can afford to drop a contract with them? In this context, irradiation can be seen to offer manufacturers a chance to regain the advantage. If you make or deal in perishable goods, a technology that leaves the goods looking fresh and fine and that extends their shelf life could be a bonus. Irradiation also offers food manufacturers a chance to intervene in some parts of the food chain where they do not at present; irradiation could give some companies a chance to gain markets in fresh food. Shelf life of vegetables and fruit could be extended to fit into new one-stop shopping patterns. Already, smaller manufacturers, producers, farmers, and retailers are being squeezed out. This process, while allowing some consumers to benefit, reduces the range of choices to many others.

Tensions between sections of the food trade are nothing new. What is new for the food business is the likelihood that by the end of the 1990s, there will be no trade barriers between the member countries of the EEC[5] and high tariff walls and quotas. There would also be uniform regulations about what is and is not acceptable for all European food, including standard rules for irradiation. This would be ideal for the big American and European companies wanting to trade in food across the EEC, but it has implications for the thousands of food workers who might lose their jobs.[6]

Clearly, the food magnates have their eyes on important matters. Big takeovers and battles for market share can lead to astronomic returns. Amid the merger mania, it is easy to forget food workers and consumers—especially those on low incomes.[7]

Thus, one answer to the question "who wants it?" could be the large manufacturers, especially those engaged in international trade between Europe and the United States and with the third world. To be able to store food longer, with an acceptable appearance of freshness, might help the processing industry's stockpile and increase its power in relation to the retailers. However, this hardly seems a compelling reason to take on irradiation technology with all its uncertainties.

Another, more compelling, reason concerns the ability of unscrupulous importers, domestic packers, and processors to conceal contamination of some foods caused by poor hygiene in handling and processing. As we saw in Chapter 5, this is already a major problem within the very small volume of trade in irradiated food that is allowed at present.

Overall, however, there is not much evidence that the food industry actually wants irradiation. Listening to the pro-irradiation lobby, we may be forgiven for thinking that the whole food industry is waiting for it with bated breath. Certainly, some of the 33 companies that established the Coalition for Food Irradiation in January 1985 may have seen it as helping their interests. However, a number of these have indicated that their participation does not imply endorsement of the process, only a desire to keep abreast of developments in the field. For example:

> Heinz does not irradiate any of its products—nor do we have any intention to do so in the foreseeable future. Our support of food irradiation to date has consisted of membership in a group that is seeking to determine, through research, if food irradiation has any long-term potential for processed food products.[8]

On the other hand, there is evidence from a British survey[9] that the food manufacturing industry is by no means united, most frequently undecided, and in many cases opposed to the use of irradiation technology at this time, for many of the reasons set out in this book.

In Britain, two of the five largest retailers; Marks & Spencer and Tesco, have indicated that they do not favor irradiation at this time, in one case because it does not fit in with the company policy of providing fresh food on a fast turnover, and in the other because of dissatisfaction with the assurances provided so far on safety. The concern from Tesco is all the more telling because that company has been involved with the British equivalent of the CFFI, a "Working Group on Food Irradiation" run by the Food Industries Research Association (FIRA) at Leatherhead in England. The British Frozen Food Federation has also expressed concern that the current ban on irradiation should not be removed.[10]

The survey we undertook in Britain followed a year-long campaign conducted through the media that attempted to convince the public that both the food industry and consumers wanted irradiation. There were statements like these:

- The food industry wants irradiation.[11]
- The food industry is optimistic that the government will give broad approval for low-level irradiation of fruit and vegetables.[12]
- Food irradiation will be ushered in by food retailers rather than manufacturers.[13]
- The Meat Trades industry is hoping for Government approval for irradiation of food.[14]
- The consumer wants fresh foods, they want long shelf life foods, they want more natural foods...this [irradiation] is a way of providing that.[15]

- There is no evidence to suggest that irradiation of food is harmful to humans.[16]
- I have a dream that for once the public will take the scientists' word and welcome the process as a great step forward.[17]

From those media quotes we get these impressions:

1. It is the food industry, and retailers in particular, who were pushing for food irradiation.

2. Consumers wanted irradiated food because it would last longer and be free from bacteria, thus making it more "safe," "natural," and "fresh."

3. The scientific community was fully convinced that there are no safety problems associated with irradiated food.

On the other hand, the feedback we had been getting from both consumers and some sections of the food industry did not support this, as the graphs of responses to the survey clearly show. The survey found only one leading company in favor of irradiation, many with reservations, and some who had already decided against it (Figure 4).

The survey also found that most of the organizations surveyed recognized a need for increased regulation and control of the technology if it is to be permitted (Table 13).

### Table 13: Issues Requiring Legislation

| Rank Area of Legislation | Respondents Indicating Need for Additional Legislation (%) |
|---|---|
| 1 Labeling | 83 |
| 2 Controls on international trade | 74 |
| 3 Worker exposure | 66 |
| 4 Registration of food premises | 59 |
| 5 Date marking of irradiated food | 55 |
| 6 Wholesomeness testing | 51 |
| 7 Nutritional labeling of foods | 47 |
| 8 Improved food hygiene regulations | 45 |
| 9 Temperature control regulations | 41 |

(Source: Reference 9.)

## Figure 4. Response to UK Survey

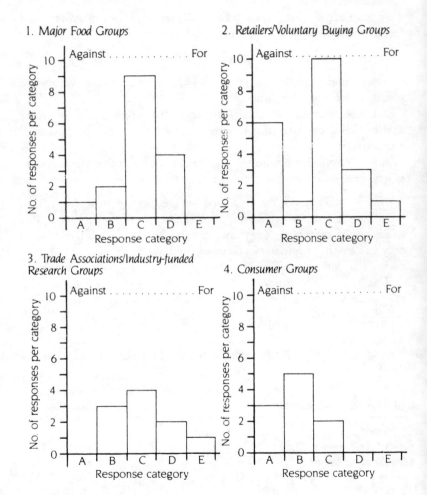

### 1. Major Food Groups
### 2. Retailers/Voluntary Buying Groups
### 3. Trade Associations/Industry-funded Research Groups
### 4. Consumer Groups

Key to Response Categories
A = Against irradiation.
B = Official policy undecided—but with reservations.
C = No official policy &/or no comment.
D = In favor, with reservations.
E = Virtually unqualified support for irradiation.

Concern was not confined to consumer organizations. Many in the industry felt these additional controls would be needed if irradiation were introduced. In addition, many industry organizations and all consumer groups felt there was a need for a public education program covering the risks and benefits of irradiation before it was introduced.[9]

These findings of widespread concern are reinforced by a survey of Trading Standards Officers throughout the United Kingdom.[18]

It seems from the London Food Commission survey that the food industry had not decided about irradiation. While some major firms in the food industry saw some benefits in irradiation, others, especially retailers and smaller producers, had reservations.

Any advantages for smaller manufacturers and retailers from the use of irradiation may well be offset by increasing their dependence on the large manufacturers, who alone can afford to invest in irradiation plants. It is also unlikely that smaller retailers can cope with consumer reaction if the large supermarket chains turn the process down.

For the farmers, as we have seen, there are no benefits. It is not they who would control the technology if it gained widespread use. They would be even more dependent on the food processors. In the case of third world farmers, there is already enough evidence to show that few have benefited from the technological advances of the so-called green revolution. The lesson is that high-level "Western" technology merely allows multinational agribusinesses to increase its control over the process of growing and marketing food on a global scale. Even if irradiation could deliver on all its technological promises, the belief that this would actually benefit those in need in poor countries is a triumph of hope over experience—a delusion that few who understand the nature of the food industry in the 20th century would subscribe to.[19]

## The Irradiation Industry?

Pressure to permit irradiation is coming from the irradiation industry.
The food industry has an interest in the process but they are very cautious. (Robert L. Lake, Chief of Regulation for the FDA Bureau of Foods, 1983).[20]

The plain fact is that pressure for food irradiation has been coming not from the food industry but from those who have already invested in irradiation plants, whether for food or for medical and other products. These companies see a bonanza if irradiation permits are given and the food industry and consumers can be persuaded to accept the process. Given the high costs and inevitable lead times before competitors could enter the field, these firms stand to make a killing if there is a rapid takeup of food irradiation.

Many public statements on the benefits of irradiation have come from people either directly involved with the irradiation industry or with close connections to it. Many of these statements also appear to be made as much with an eye on the stock market value of the companies as to the effect on public opinion. In several instances, they also appear to be part of the campaign by these companies to influence government decisions to permit irradiation.

In Britain, statements on the benefits of food irradiation were linked throughout 1985 to hints that the government advisory committee was about to give the process its approval. A similar pattern emerges from analysis of the press reports from the United States. There, as reported in the press, two major irradiation firms linked the benefits of the process with impending approval by the FDA.

In Britain, a small working group on food irradiation was set up at Leatherhead with representatives of the following companies: Isotron, the company with a virtual monopoly position in the field of gamma irradiation facilities capable of handling food; Radiation Dynamics, the leading user of electron beam and x-ray sterilization techniques; Unilever plc, one of the major food companies with strong Dutch connections; and the Leatherhead Food Industries Research Association.

Two of the leading British spokespersons on the advantages of food irradiation quoted in the media have been Alan Holmes of Leatherhead and Frank Ley of Isotron.

Frank Ley has worked in the food research department at Unilever and as principal scientific officer at the United Kingdom Atomic Energy Authority, leading a team investigating the irradiation of food. In 1970, he left to set up a private irradiation company.[21] In September 1983, Ley, now the marketing director of Isotron and a leading shareholder in it, was appointed as industrial advisor to the Advisory Committee.

Several British Members of Parliament introduced a motion in the

House of Commons pointing out their concern over possible conflict of interest (see Appendix 2). Specifically, they noted that predictions of the main recommendation of the Advisory Committee had been widely leaked, not least by Frank Ley; that the company had raised capital through a flotation on the stock exchange, while the committee was sitting, to build a new irradiation plant (Isotron already had existing production spare capacity of 46% at its four existing plants);[22] and that there had been a rise in the capital value of Isotron when stories in the financial press linked the future of the company to the impending recommendations of the Advisory Committee. The motion called for an investigation of share dealings in the company (see Appendix 2).[23]

Clearly, it does not help public acceptance of the impartiality of the Advisory Committee report to have suggestions of conflict of interest. This would be of little consequence if the scientific evidence put forward by the report were impeccable and verifiable. As we have shown, this is far from the case.

There have also been difficulties with the development of the food and radiation industry in the United States. Analysis of press reports in the United States indicates that the most vocal spokesperson for food irradiation has undoubtedly been Martin Welt, former president of Radiation Technology, Inc. Radiation Technology has four plants in New Jersey, Virginia, North Carolina, and Arkansas. One of them was the subject of scandal when its license was revoked in 1986. Various reports quoting Welt throughout 1983 hinted that the FDA was about to give clearances for foods that Radiation Technology had petitioned for permission to irradiate. The other major company in the news in 1983 was Isomedix. It now has a network of eleven irradiation facilities in seven states, Puerto Rico, and Ontario, Canada. In July the company raised about $16 million in capital through a share flotation to finance the cost of expansion, including construction of an additional three facilities.[24]

In April 1984, the Securities and Exchange Commission of the New York Stock Exchange uncovered insider trading involving the shares of both Radiation Technology and Isomedix, linked to favorable reports on both companies in the *Wall Street Journal*.[25] Martin Welt, though not implicated in illegal share dealings, was required to resign as president of Radiation Technology, Inc., in 1986 by the NRC in order to obtain a license reinstatement for Rockaway plant. He remains a major shareholder.[26]

## "Atoms for Peace"—The Role of the Nuclear Industry

Even this level of corporate vested interest does not explain the international pressures. Food processors and irradiation companies are clearly opportunist, but they are not the prime motivators of the international program that is currently selling the benefits of food irradiation and systematically ensuring its acceptance on a global scale.

To understand these pressures, we need to go back to the origins of the technology in the "atoms for peace" program of the 1950s. This was taken up internationally through the IAEA and by a joint committee with the WHO and FAO as early as 1961.[27] As we have seen, the IAEA has spent a considerable portion of its budget on promoting the international scientific consensus on the benefits and safety of irradiation as a food processing technology. The latest phase of this program involves systematic promotion of approvals for the process by governments and key organizations that can influence public opinion.

In the United States we have seen that it is the DOE—the agency responsible for most of the nuclear energy and weapons industry plants—that is providing at least $10 million to finance demonstration food irradiation plants using cesium 137 rather than the potentially more economic, efficient, and versatile x-ray technology.

Why? If the benefits are as great as claimed, why the need for the hard sell? Who else stands to benefit?

The main gamma ray source used worldwide for food irradiation is cobalt 60. It is manufactured by placing nonradioactive cobalt 59 in the core of a nuclear reactor for about 18 months. The process is carried out by only a handful of nuclear power companies. Atomic Energy of Canada, Ltd. (AECL), produces about 90% of the world's industrial cobalt. The supply has been outstripped by demand in recent years, and AECL has had to draw up an allocation schedule. The company is planning to increase production threefold, with a new facility near Ottawa, but even so, the supply is unlikely to be sufficient to meet a rapid rise in demand such as that we would experience if food irradiation were to gain widespread acceptance.

In these circumstances, the alternative isotope, cesium 137, becomes an attractive proposition, even though the gamma rays it emits are of a lower energy level and, as we have seen, it may be more dangerous to handle. But, what is the source of cesium? Again, it is a byproduct of nuclear reactor technology, this time produced mainly as a fission product in spent fuel rods—in other words, a highly radioactive waste product and one which, because of its 30-year half-life, poses serious problems for those trying to find a solution for the disposal of nuclear wastes. It is the cesium wastes that the DOE is most eager to find a use for. Could it be that the whole program to promote food irradiation is little more than a thinly disguised attempt to find a commercial use for radioactive wastes? This hardly seems plausible; yet, the early texts on food irradiation make exactly this kind of connection.[28] Since then, food irradiation has taken on a life of its own, but the original pressures remain, and perhaps help to explain some of the irrational behavior of the agencies promoting it.

There is currently no reprocessing of commercial spent nuclear fuel in the United States. What reprocessing occurs is done to extract plutonium for the nuclear weapons program. France and Britain, however, do undertake reprocessing, at the Sellafield plant in Cumbria and The Cap La Hague plant on the Brittany coast. In addition, for both the United States and Europe, there is the possibility that radioactive cobalt, also produced as a waste product by the activation of the cobalt in the steam generators of pressurized water reactors, might be worth refining commercially to meet a shortfall in demand for radioactive sources if food irradiation facilities were to be built in large numbers.

Even if there is no direct benefit to the nuclear industry from disposal of problematic nuclear wastes, there are clearly benefits to the image of the "atoms for peace" program from having another "beneficial" use of radiation. Who can dispute that the beleaguered nuclear industry urgently needs a boost to its tattered image in this decade that has seen Three Mile Island, Chernobyl, growing evidence of childhood leukemias around the British reprocessing plants at Sellafield and Dounreay, and not a single new order for a nuclear power plant in the United States since 1978?

However, the underlying concern of many who have monitored the activities of the nuclear industry over the years is that the artificially created need for cesium may be used to justify reprocessing of spent commercial fuel in the United States, thereby making the civilian plutonium available for the production of even more nuclear weapons.

## Consumers

Even if it is a little unclear who might want irradiation and what their underlying motives might be, it is very clear that consumers don't. Studies of consumer attitudes have been done and show that consumers overwhelmingly do not want irradiated food.[29,30,31,32,33]

Perhaps most embarrassing of all has been the fact that their reaction is not just one of confusing irradiation of food with radioactive food. Several studies have found that the more educated the consumer, the more information they have (even when this information is provided by the industry lobby), and the higher their economic and social status, the less they want irradiation.[30,31,34]

The figures are not marginal. In most surveys, 65 to 95% of people are regularly classified as opposed to irradiation, even when the most favorable light is put on the figures.

There has been no national poll of opinion in the United States on irradiation of food. In Britain, a national opinion poll was conducted for the London Food Commission by the Marplan Polling Organization. This poll found that until there was a test to detect irradiated food,

- 93% thought the current ban should not be removed at this time.
- 95% thought all food (including ingredients) should be labeled.
- 85% would not buy irradiated food even if the government removed the ban.[31]

This consumer reaction cannot be dismissed as ignorance or the product of "scaremongering" by the critics of irradiation. In many cases, it is based on quite widespread understanding of what irradiation is and does and some of the problems it creates for the consumer and the food industry.[30,31,34,35]

As the director of the European Consumers' group BEUC put it simply to the head of the EEC's Foodstuffs Division:

> If consumers don't want it are you saying that the EEC will force the member countries to use it?[36]

It is true that some people will be confused and think that irradiated might mean radioactive. We will be out there along with irradiation's proponents, explaining that it is not, and that the issues are not the same. It is not in our interests to have the public view this issue in any other than the terms we have set out in this book—issues of food safety, quality, and wholesomeness; the controllability of the technology; and a serious consideration of areas where it is really needed. If there is any confusion between irradiation and other nuclear issues, then we respectfully suggest that those who oversell the case for irradiation and who override public concern have only themselves to blame.[35]

Perhaps the most telling question in the British poll was the one asking who people would believe (Table 14).

Clearly there is widespread mistrust on this issue. We suggest that this has much to do with the past record of various organizations, leading to their forfeiting the public trust on this as with other issues of concern.

### Table 14: Percentage Saying They Would Buy Irradiated Foods If They Were Told It Was Safe By

| | |
|---|---|
| Government | 25% |
| Food industry scientists | 29% |
| Food manufacturers | 16% |
| Nuclear industry | 12% |
| Consumers' organizations | 40% |

(Source: Reference 31.)

## Conclusion

We began by seeing food irradiation as a food processing technology with potential benefits, especially in the area of replacing some hazardous chemicals and pesticides used to control insect infestations in fruit and spices. As we uncovered the facts, we became increasingly disturbed that there was more to this issue than appeared on the surface. There were, in fact, serious questions still to be answered and what appear to be vested interests and hidden motives among those pushing for irradiation.

We have now reached the conclusion that these forces need to be opposed. The facts we have laid before you raise issues of concern in all four areas:

- The safety of irradiated foods.
- The wholesomeness of foods that have been irradiated, and the consumers' rights to information.
- Whether this technology can be controlled at the present time in the absence of appropriate tests and in the face of clear evidence of abuse in the international food trade, and whether we can provide adequate controls on worker safety and the radioactive pollution of the environment.
- Finally, whether it is in fact needed; or whether it is a technology looking for a use with arguments invented and pushed on governments, the food industry, and consumers by those who stand to gain financially or who have other agendas.

These issues need to be dealt with, whether we proceed with irradiation or not. They are as important for those who are in favor of food irradiation as they are for those who are against. For the many who have yet to decide, they are crucial.

---

REFERENCES

1. *Marketing Guidelines for Acceptance and Usage of Food Irradiation.* Task Force on Marketing and Public Relations of the International Consultative group on Food Irradiation (ICGFI), Vienna, September 15-19, 1986.
2. Joint FAO/IAEA Division of Isotope and Radiation Applications of Atomic Energy for Food and Agriculture Development. *Food Irradiation Newsletter*, Vol. 10, No. 2, IAEA, Vienna, November 1986.
3. J. M. Connor, R. J. Rogers, B. W. Marion, and W. F. Mueller. *The Food Manufacturing Industries: Structure, Strategies, Performance and Policies.* Lexington, Massachusetts: Lexington Books, 1985.
4. I. Cole-Hamilton and T. Lang. *Tightening Belts.* London Food Commission, London, 1986.
5. Lord Cockfield. Memorandum: Completion of the Internal Market (COM [85]), 310, and Community Legislation on Foodstuffs (COM [85] 603). EEC, Brussels, 1986.
6. Bakers, Food and Allied Workers Union. Comments on ACINF. Welwyn Garden City, UK, July 1986.

7. LFC letters to UK NEDO Food and Drink Manufacturing EDC, March 1986, and to the UK Monopolies and Mergers Commission, February 1986.
8. Donna Elliott, Manager, Consumer Relations Heinz USA, in letter to Betsy Russ, CAIR, October 23, 1986.
9. Tony Webb and Angela Henderson. *Food Irradiation—Who Wants It?* London Food Commission, London, 1986.
10. Statement of BFFF position 1986. Reproduced in *Food Irradiation: The Facts.* London: Thorsons, 1987.
11. *The Observer* (London), 5 May 1985.
12. *The Sunday Times* (London), 4 August 1985.
13. *Supermarketing* (London), 29 November 1985.
14. *Meat Trades Journal* (London), 20 March 1986.
15. Alan Holmes, Food Industry Research Association Spokesperson, on BBC Radio 4, London, 5 June 1985.
16. Sir Arnold Burgen, Chairman of ACINF. *Observer,* 5 May 1985. (A year before the ACINF report was published.)
17. Alan Holmes. *Daily Express* (London), 4 February 1985.
18. Survey of Trading Standards Officers by London Borough of Haringey, 1986.
19. Susan George. How the Other Half Die. London: Penguin, 1975. Frances Moore-Lappe and J. Collins. *Food First.* New York: Ballantine, 1979.
20. Quotes in Heard on the Street, Support for Food Irradiation May Dim. *Wall Street Journal,* January 31, 1983.
21. Isotron plc. Offer for Sale by Tender of 3,290,088 Ordinary Shares of 25p Each at Minimum Tender Price of 120p Per Share. J. Henry Schroder Wagg and Co., London, 27 June 1985.
22. *Financial Times* (London), January 7, 1985; *Daily Telegraph* (London), January 7, 1985. House of Commons Motion, Great Britain, April 9, 1986, No. 713, by Skinner, Lloyd, Caborn, Sedgemore, Litherhead, and Ross.
23. Irradiated Foods: Conflict of Interest. Early Day Motion, House of Commons Order Paper, London, April 9, 1986.
24. *Wall Street Journal,* 13 May 1983, 5 July 1983, 6 July 1983, 18 August 1983, 19 March 1984. *DJ News,* 7 October 1983, 29 December 1983, 20 April 1984, 6 June 1984, 22 June 1984, 25 June 1984, 30 July 1984, 17 October 1984, 9 November 1984, 12 November 1984, 30 November 1984, 2 January 1985, 17 July 1985, 17 October 1985, 20 January 1986.
25. Investor Traded in 6 Issues Before News Appeared in Wall Street Journal. *Wall Street Journal,* 6 April 1984. Also, The Wall Street Journal has Reported Some Details of M. David Clark's Share Dealing. *International Herald Tribune,* 7 April 1984.
26. 51 Federal Register 23612, June 30, 1986. Robin Lally. NRC Removes Him, DOE Gets Him. *Daily Record* (Morris West, NJ), September 25, 1986, B1.
27. Dr. F. K. Kaferstein. Food Safety Program, WHO. The Role of WHO in the Field of Food Irradiation. Statement, 4 March 1985, to International Symposium on Food Irradiation Processing, Washington, DC, 1985.

28. R. S. Hannan. *Scientific and Technical Problems Involved in Using Ionizing Radiations for the Preservation of Food.* Dept. of Scientific and Industrial Research, Food Investigation Special Report No. 61, London: HMSO, 1955.

29. Titlebaum, Dubin, and Doyle. Will Consumers Accept Irradiated Foods. *Journal of Food Safety,* 5, 219-228, 1983, and Bruhn, Schultz and Sommer. Attitude Change Toward Food Irradiation Among Conventional and Alternative Consumers. *Food Technology,* January 1986.

30. Denise Rennie, et. al. Presentation to Seminar on Food Irradiation, Salford University, UK, 1986.

31. *Food Irradiation.* Omnibus Research by Marplan Ltd. Conducted for the London Food Commission, London, January 1987.

32. Brand Group. *Irradiated Seafood Products: A Position Paper for the Seafood Industry.* Prepared for the National Marine Fisheries Service, Washington, DC, January 1986.

33. Consumer Interpol Memo. International Organization of Consumers' Unions (IOCU), Penang, Malaysia, August 1986.

34. Survey conducted by the UK Consumers' Association, London, November 1986.

35. HIS Associates. Irradiation of Foods: Prototype Study in Conveying Health-risk Issues. Submitted to Center for Food Safety and Applied Nutrition, Division of Consumer Studies, FDA, Washington, DC, June 1986.

36. Tony Venables, Director of BEUC. One Day Seminar, Food Irradiation—Assessing Risks and Benefits. IEHO, London, January 1987.

# CHAPTER 8

# PRESSURE POINTS

WITH THE PRESSURES for irradiation at both national and international levels, it will be necessary for the public to speak clearly and with determination.

As we have seen, there are issues that should concern the most ardent supporters of irradiation as much as its opponents, and that will certainly concern many who are as yet undecided.

If you are eager to see that these issues are considered, we hope you will take action. Such is the nature of democracy. We hope that what follows will help you in deciding where to apply pressure so that the real concerns of those who will be affected by the decision to allow irradiation of food are heard.

## The Scientific Community

One of the main pillars of the pro-irradiation lobby's case is that the process has been declared safe by some very eminent organizations. Yet, as we have seen, the case for the safety of irradiated foods is in fact very weak. There are many unanswered questions. These may not, in the final analysis, be grounds for declaring the process unsafe, but they do require answers—real, honest, scientific answers based on fact, not opinions. "Trust us, we are the experts" will not do. We need to urge the scientific community to demand a fuller, more open investigation of the evidence and encourage academics and scientists to contribute to the debate on the risks as well as the benefits of irradiation.

In Britain, perhaps because there is a ban on irradiation that requires a conscious decision to overturn it, the medical community has been far more critical than in the United States. One really has to ask how it is that the American Medical Association (AMA) can endorse the process when their British counterparts (the BMA) are producing a report highly critical of the safety of the process.

The AMA states:

> Many years of international experience have demonstrated that food irradiation at levels of up to one megarad is a safe process. Food irradiation produces no significant reduction in the nutritional quality of food. Moreover, it has a number of important potential applications. Food irradiation holds the promise of being a viable alternative to the pesticide ethylene dibromide in the post-harvest disinfestation of fruits and vegetables. It may also be used to control *Salmonella* in red meats, poultry, and fish. In addition, food irradiation could extend the storage life of numerous perishable foods.[1]

In contrast, the BMA's Board of Science report is highly critical of the British ACINF report, which it says

> may not sufficiently take account of, still less exclude, possible long term medical effects on the population, given that irradiated products have been available for a relatively short period of time.

According to the BMA,

> more scientific data is required...and a full scale study should be undertaken...before the process can be confidently accepted.[2]

Within the scientific community there is a code of ethics: a sense that what is done in the name of science needs to be done openly and subjected to independent scrutiny, review, and criticism.

For the lay person faced with "experts," it is sufficient to ask the questions and demand to see the evidence.

## The Congress

We often fail to recognize that behind every person who writes a letter to his or her Senator or Congressperson, there stand a hundred or more who are equally concerned but do not write. Corporate interests may be able to hire lobbyists, offer financial contributions, and press their case within the corridors of power, but it is the people who elect and defeat the Congressional representatives. Enough mail on an issue assures that it is given careful attention. Enough mail requesting specific action means that action will probably follow.

The bills before both houses of Congress in the names of Congressman Douglas Boscoe (D-CA) and Senator George Mitchell (D-ME) make specific proposals that would prevent the government from implementing regulations, passed since 1985, permitting irradiation of foods. Their proposals would also block further development of food irradiation, for the time being, and demand further studies on these issues:

1. Health effects of eating irradiated foods.
2. Environmental consequences of transportation of radioactive material.
3. Worker health and safety.
4. Accident and emergency planning and risks to local populations from irradiation plants.
5. Responsibilities for cleanup of any contamination.

These bills would also require consumer labeling of irradiated foods in stores and restaurants, and control import and export of foods not approved for domestic consumption.

Details of Congressman Boscoe's bill are given in Appendix 4. Letters of support can be sent to Congressman Boscoe and Senator Mitchell, but, more importantly, your own representatives can be asked to co-sponsor and vote for these bills.

## The Federal Agencies

Much of the detailed application of legislation in the United States is left to the agencies involved. As we have seen, responsibilities are shared between the FDA—for approvals of uses of irradiation—and the USDA—for regulation of irradiated meat products.

In addition, the Bureau of Standards at the Department of Commerce is involved in developing tests. The DOE is funding "demonstration" irradiation facilities, and the NRC is licensing irradiation facilities.

Thousands of letters and petitions from consumers and their organizations in 1984-85 forced the FDA to include a labeling requirement in the final rule. Currently, there is a letter-writing campaign to force the FDA to schedule hearings on its decision to permit irradiation up to 100,000 rad (1 kGy). If this fails, several organizations will take the issue into the federal courts and test the legality of the decisions.

Concerned supporters of more open decision-making can help by writing to the FDA and sending copies of their letters to the Health and Energy Institute (HEI), Public Citizen (PC), or the Environmental Policy Institute (EPI). Addresses for these organizations are given in Appendix 5.

The USDA has appeared more willing than the FDA to listen to consumer concerns. The Coalition for Alternatives in Nutrition and Healthcare (CANAH) organized a meeting between concerned groups and USDA staff. Letters to the USDA with comments in support of the department's position on the risks of botulism food poisoning from vacuum packaging of irradiated meats, and concern over the decision to permit irradiation of pork and on the awaited decision on poultry can have impact on the USDA's decision-making process.

The role of the Department of Energy in the promotion of food irradiation calls for public investigation. The plan for six demonstration irradiators appears to have more to do with utilization of nuclear waste, and creating a climate for separation of plutonium as well as cesium from civilian nuclear reactor fuel, than with any concern over public health or food safety. These DOE facilities can bypass the NRC licensing system. Despite DOE assurances that this would not occur,[3] as of February 1987, the NRC had no record of an application for a license for any of its DOE food irradiation facilities.[4]

Congressional representatives should be urged to question the DOE's activities and insist that any federally funded demonstration projects for irradiators be based on the best technical and economic alternatives (unlikely to be cesium 137) and subject to full licensing and control. Once the DOE plans are known, concerned citizens will need to question the granting of local and state permits (see State and Local Government, below).

The NRC licenses the facilities using cobalt 60 or cesium 137 and regulates them unless there is an agreement with the host state. Lack of funding prevents effective enforcement by the NRC of even the best regulations at existing facilities—let alone any new food irradiators. It is important for local citizens to demand public hearings over any commercial irradiation plants and to challenge any proposals to amend licenses of existing plants to allow irradiation of food.

As well as the food irradiation plants (Table 3 page 18), we include a list of some of the other irradiation plants in the United States in Appendix 1. Some of these might be capable of irradiating food.

## Other Agencies

The Office of Management and Budget became involved in the food irradiation controversy when former Secretary of Health and Human Services Margaret Heckler tried to clear the way for irradiated foods to be labeled not as irradiated but as "picowaved".[5] Heckler's attempt to rush this through before leaving office, and the deluge of protesting calls to the OMB, forced the agency to institute a review of the regulations. The FDA was asked for new economic impact analyses, and discussions led to withdrawal of "picowaved" in favor of the Radura symbol and the word "irradiated".[6]

It is possible that citizen pressure could force the Environmental Protection Agency to become involved in demands for an Environmental Impact Assessment (EIA) for irradiation plants.

## State and Local Government

State and local government officials are often more accessible and responsive to citizen concerns. The City Council of New York adopted a resolution opposing the proposed FDA regulation in 1984, and several other cities and counties did the same in response to citizen pressure and concern.

So far, most of the pressure has been for labeling of irradiated foods. The state of Vermont passed a bill in 1986 that requires irradiated foods to be labeled "Treated with Radiation" and establishes fines for violations.[7] The campaign to ensure labeling was launched by the Vermont Alliance to Protect Our Food (VAPOF) and the Vermont Public Interest Research Group (VPIRG).

Legislation to require labeling has been introduced in several other states, including Oregon, Minnesota, and New York. In Santa Cruz, California, legislation introduced by Food Irradiation Response (FIR) was passed in 1986, requiring food retailers to post notices adjacent to any food known to have been irradiated.

The other main area for public pressure has been further study. In California, Senate Joint Resolution 58, introduced by Senator Milton Marks, passed on August 28, 1986. SJR 58 asks the Secretary of Health and Human Services to study extensively the risk to human health and the environment and to suspend any new food irradiation approvals pending the study outcome.[8]

More recently, organizers are seeking outright bans on irradiated foods. In May 1987, the nation's first bill banning the sale and distribution of irradiated food was signed into state law in Maine.[9] The efforts of the group People for Responsible Management of Radioactive Waste, resulted in the New Jersey State Senate passing a bill to ban distribution of irradiated foods, except for spices, in New Jersey in February 1987. The Senate vote was 30 to 3 in favor of banning irradiated food.[10] The bill will become law if passed by the Assembly.

For areas where irradiation facilities exist or are planned, local and state zoning, environmental, and land use laws can be consulted as possible means to prevent or close down irradiators.

Union County, New Jersey, passed a nuclear free zone ordinance to prevent the siting of a Radiation Technology plant within its boundaries. The ordinance was overturned in a court challenge by the company. The county is now exploring other legal avenues to prevent the facility. The siting of another facility in Port Elizabeth, New Jersey, was also prevented by organized community efforts.[11]

Radiation Technology plans to site an irradiator in the Milwaukee, Wisconsin, area were foiled by local opposition from both business owners and residents.[12] Radiation Technology announced in January 1987 that it "could build a facility for less money in other areas of the country, where there is less opposition".[13]

California citizens also mounted successful campaigns to prevent the siting of irradiation facilities in three separate communities.[11]

## Industry Pressure Points

As we saw in Chapter 6, the food industry is by no means united in wanting food irradiation. There is an underlying struggle for power between processors and retailers. While irradiation might offer advantages to some processors, there are also benefits to be gained from clear statements of policy opposing irradiation at this time. We would argue that responsible food companies should be in the forefront of the campaign for a moratorium on irradiation until there are tests that can detect irradiation, so that consumer choice can be guaranteed and the existing abuses stamped out.

In Britain, the national Food and Drink Federation (FDF), representing the major food companies, has stated that it is no longer seeking a removal of the ban on irradiated food in Britain until such time as tests are developed that can detect irradiation. This follows earlier statements from the British Frozen Food Federation, the Farmers Union, and two of the leading supermarket chains.[14]

Some companies in the United States have already taken a position. Arrowhead Mills, which produces organic foods in northern Texas, has promised that it "will not use (or allow to be used) any form of irradiation on the foods it sells." Citizen groups are eliciting the stance of other food companies, and eventually hope to extract similar promises from all of them.

Some leading food companies have joined with the irradiation companies to form the Coalition for Food Irradiation. As of February 13, 1986, members included Alpo Petfoods, Inc., American Meat Institute, Beatrice Companies, Inc., CH2M Hill, Campbell Soup Co., W. R. Grace & Co., Del Monte Corp., E. I. du Pont de Nemours & Co., Inc., Emergent Technologies, Inc., Rockwell International, Gaines Foods, Inc., General Foods, George A. Hormel & Co., Gerber Products Co., Heinz USA, Hershey Foods Corp., Isomedix, Inc., Kraft, Inc., Mars, Inc., McCormick & Co., Inc., National Food Processors Association, National Pork Producers Council, Northwest Horticultural Council, Oscar Mayer Foods Corp., Papaya Administrative Comm., Produce Marketing Association, Ralston Purina Co., Sandoz Nutrition, Stokely USA Inc., Stouffer Foods Corp., Thomas J. Lipton Co., United Fresh Fruit and Vegetable Association, and Welch Foods Inc.[15]*

While this body seeks to promote the benefits of irradiation, it is clear from correspondence with these companies that not all of the coalition members are intending to use the process. As a Thomas J. Lipton spokesperson wrote in November 1986:

> We recognize that there is a great deal of confusion associated with food irradiation. Therefore we are participating in the Coalition for Food Irradiation, a group comprised of scientists, food industry representatives and consumer advocates. We hope that through this coalition, we will better understand the advantages and disadvantages of food irradiation as well as any concerns regarding

---

*Since this list was compiled, a number of these companies have withdrawn their membership from the coalition for Food Irradiation, indicating that companies can be influenced by consumer opinion.

> its use. At present, Lipton does not irradiate any food products. We are not involved in any food irradiation research, nor is any planned.[16]

It is not clear which "consumer advocates" Lipton is referring to. As far as we are aware, no responsible consumer advocate is in favor of irradiation at this time.

It is important that people write to food companies, especially those involved in the Coalition for Food Irradiation, to find out exactly where they stand and to let them know of the widespread nature of the public concern and of the full range of issues that concern critics of the process. Many people in the food industry have been convinced that safety is the only issue and that this has been settled by the various expert bodies. Citizens Against Irradiated Food (CAIR), based in Ohio, wrote to food processors to elicit information about their current and planned irradiation practices, and received answers from 44 companies (see Appendix 3). Only McCormick replied that it was irradiating products, although not for direct retail sales (which would require a label to consumers). Beatrice-Hunt/Wesson admitted that it had used irradiated spices, but several companies did not respond to the inquiry regarding the use of irradiated ingredients. Campbell Soup Co., Heinz, McCormick, and Gerber wrote that they are conducting research into food irradiation. Several companies considered the technology promising or safe (Beatrice-Hunt/Wesson, Campbell's Soup Company, Carnation, R. T. French Co., Holsum Foods, Thomas J. Lipton, Inc., and Ralston Purina).[17]

The majority of manufacturers do not yet use irradiated foods, and most have taken no position regarding the process. Hormel stated that consumer acceptance of irradiated foods is a "crucial issue." "Unless consumers are willing to purchase irradiated foods, grocers will not stock them and food processors will not invest in the technology".[18] Labeling is critical. If consumers do not know that their food or food ingredients were irradiated, then the problem of consumer rejection can be avoided. Manufacturers can then be more certain that the major food stores will carry irradiated products.

United States grocers and supermarket chains are apparently taking a more cautious approach to food irradiation. When Isomedix test-marketed irradiated mangoes in the fall of 1986, the major food chains·

refused to carry the product in Florida.[19] Store picketing in Southern California in spring 1987 also stopped test-marketing of irradiated papayas.[20] The lesson from Britain is that one of the most sensitive pressure points in any country is the large retail companies. None of them is likely to declare in favor of irradiation and risk losing trade to its competitors. At the same time, there may be a commercial advantage to be derived from an early decision not to use irradiation technology. The British and Canadian Marks & Spencer Companies have stated that they intend to maintain their policy of "providing quality fresh food on a fast turnover" and so had no use for irradiation. There are a variety of ways that consumers can exert pressure on supermarkets to join the call for a halt to irradiation at this time, e.g., letters to the company president, leafleting and petition-collecting outside selected supermarkets, and encouraging customers to hand in model letters and cards at the checkout counter and to add their own comments in letters to the company. In the event that some supermarket chains introduce irradiated foods, some people might even consider organizing consumer boycotts.

Health food stores were among the first to oppose irradiation. Santa Rosa Community Foods wrote the FDA regarding food irradiation:

> In essence, we feel that until the longterm safety questions are answered, it is dangerous to allow use of this process. What we find more important, as consumers and as distributors of foods, is the proposal not to label irradiated foods as such....As responsible business people we demand that you require accurate labeling of all foods exposed to the irradiation process, through all the generations that that food product is used.[21]

At the same time, some health food stores are merely part of large corporations, and these need to be pressed to take a clear stand on the issue and to help local campaigns by distributing material calling attention to the issues of concern. Petitions opposing food irradiation and demanding consumer labeling have been circulated by some health food stores and food co-ops. These were used both to educate consumers about the potential hazard and to advise the FDA that consumers believed that the FDA was making a mistake.

On the other hand, food irradiation promoters like the American Spice Trade Association wrote the FDA that they were "encouraged...

by the absence of a labeling requirement for retail products."[22] The Almond Board of California warned the FDA, "In fact, a special retail label could be damaging ..."[23]

Robert Turner, International Promotion Director of the Washington State Apple Commission, wrote the FDA:

> It is not necessary to add the irradiation of the foodstuff to the existing label, or to create a new label identifying food irradiation. In the case of possibly irradiated fresh apples for insect control, the irradiation process could be compared to the washing and waxing processes of apples which are also not identified on any label attached to the fresh apples.[24]

The FDA April 1986 rule completely eliminated "food ingredients" from labeling requirements, thereby exempting the irradiation of any food item, once combined with another, from being brought to the attention of consumers.[6] Dropping the wording from labels in April 1988, and using only the "Radura" flower symbol on whole foods, would leave most consumers unaware that their food had been irradiated. It is clear that some sections of the food industry are eager to prevent consumer knowledge of irradiation, so as to prevent refusal in the marketplace.

Boycotts of companies irradiating foods are under consideration by some groups, with McCormick frequently being suggested as a target, since they admit to irradiating food ingredients (spices) that are not labeled to the public. If certain imported items, like papayas, become the test food for irradiation, consumers will be urged to boycott all papayas, in case food suppliers refuse to supply the necessary labels.

Even if labeling is made mandatory, enforcement will be a problem. The FDA has admitted, "We cannot tell you at this time how often each local grocery store will be inspected to determine compliance or noncompliance with the labeling requirements" regarding irradiated foods.[25] Local health officials say they do not have the personnel to check grocery stores, which they usually only visit once a year. There are only 21 FDA offices, scattered in major cities, so they are unlikely to be able to police stores regarding labeling.

## Farmers

Farm organizations are potential allies in the campaign to prevent-needless food irradiation. Application of food irradiation at the farm does not seem feasible. Even the promoters of food irradiation have admitted that irradiated food will be more expensive. Farmers are often blamed for rising food prices, when the benefactors of the price rises are processors and distributors, not the farmers. In addition, the ability to stockpile foods such as grain for longer time periods could adversely affect farm sales of new crops.

Farm organizations have already been approached with claims that food irradiation will help the farmer, and some groups have believed these claims. The American Farm Bureau Federation represents more than 3.3 million member families, who help produce virtually every commodity in the United States. John C. Datt, Secretary and Director of the Farm Bureau, wrote the FDA in 1984, stating:

> Agribusiness must be allowed to use the most modern technological advances if we are to continue to be able to provide consumers with the most wholesome food products at the most affordable prices. While we approve of FDA's authorization of the use of the irradiation food process, we are not necessarily advocating its use. Once the technology is available, its use will be determined on a commodity by commodity basis.[26]

The National Pork Producers Council has promoted pork irradiation very actively.[27] Many of their state chapters wrote to the FDA supporting irradiation, and the group lobbied for construction of food irradiators for pork. Despite recent regulations approving pork irradiation to control trichinae, no one was using the process as of spring 1987. In fact, Dr. David Meeker, staff scientist for the National Pork Producers Council, told the NCSFI that "it is more useful to test for trichina than to irradiate 100% of pork to get at the 0.6% [that might be infected.]"[27,28]

Apparently, the National Pork Producers Council wanted to insure that all trichina control options were kept open, rather than switch the industry to that particular technology. Their initial support for irradiation helped promote the DOE project destined for Ames, Iowa, which is intended to irradiate pork. This project will provide a taxpayer subsidy for processing, but no major meat companies have invested in their own facilities yet.

In Britain, farmers' and growers' organizations are opposed to the introduction of irradiation. Farm groups who support food irradiation should be asked to reconsider, and those that have not taken a position asked to review the hazards and oppose the process.

## Unions

Food handlers in a variety of industries may eventually be expected to become involved in or work near food irradiators, so food workers are a natural constituency for concerns about worker safety. Workers are also consumers. Since all union members need to eat and feed their families, all unions can be asked to consider this issue.

The Food and Allied Service Trades Department (FAST) of the AFL/CIO has taken the view outlined earlier in this book that irradiation should be studied as a possible substitute for more toxic chemicals in the disinfestation of fruit, but it is doubtful about its use as a way of preserving food. As Debbie Berkowitz, FAST Health and Safety Director, has said:

> It is unclear whether any benefits in this area outweigh the risks to workers and consumers. We are, like our British Trade Union colleagues, deeply concerned about the worker safety aspects and feel the whole issue needs further study before any widespread employment of irradiation technology. In addition, our members being consumers and residents, we also have deep concerns about consumer risks from consumption of irradiated foods and transport of highly radioactive materials around the country.[29]

American labor unions have been in the forefront of some campaigns about the transportation of radioactive materials.

In Britain, the Food Irradiation Campaign has the endorsement of several key national unions involved in the food trade, including the Transport and General Workers (T & GWU), General Municipal and Boilermakers (GMB), Bakery Food and Allied Workers (BFAWU), The Union of Shop Distributive and Allied Workers (USDAW), and the National Union of Public Employees (NUPE). Internationally, the European Committee of Food Catering and

Allied Workers Union within the International Union of Foodworkers (ECF-IUF) has insisted that

> Techno-physiological processes should only be used when, first they present no health hazards and secondly when they are technically indispensable.[30]

And on consumer protection in general, it states:

> The ECF has considerable reservations in this field as to whether consumers really can be protected against insidious deterioration in quality and fraudulent practices through labeling obligations and the recognition of quality brands.[30]

There is considerable scope for raising many of the concerns about irradiation through the labor movement. A resolution was passed at the California state Labor Federation of the AFL/CIO in 1986, opposing food irradiation, supporting the Bosco bill, and demanding honest consumer labeling if food irradiation is to be allowed in the future.[31] Similar resolutions have already been passed by many local unions around the country, but more are needed. This local union pressure can be used to alert the international unions to the concern of their members and can be used as part of the campaigns for legislation at municipal, county, state, and federal government levels. Unions need to be alerted to the proposals in the IAEA/FAO international marketing strategy that suggest co-opting some trade union leaders onto the national steering committees promoting food irradiation technology.[32] It is not in labor's interest to be associated with such pressures, but rather to be seen calling for further study, greater safeguards, and a halt to further developments until the many issues of concern have been resolved.

## Consumer Organizing

The National Coalition to Stop Food Irradiation, based in California, whose address is given in Appendix 5, serves as an umbrella organization for many of the opponents of the process in the United States. Local chapters and affiliated organizations in most areas of the country can be reached through the NCSFI.

Campaign efforts are being undertaken at local and national levels to educate Congress, federal agencies, food processors, food distributors, the press, and the general public about the potential hazards of the process and to assert the right of consumers to know how their food has been treated by requiring an honest label. A great deal of effort goes into tracking food irradiation activities by both industry and government and raising the concerns at public meetings, some of which are those organized by the Coalition for Food Irradiation in its attempt to promote the technology.

Since everybody eats, most organizations can add food irradiation to the list of their members' concerns. As individuals learn about the potential hazards of this process, they can bring this issue to groups in which they are already members.

A couple of examples may help illustrate what can be done. Roberta Kopstein and Rebecca Kirschbaum, both of New Jersey, did just that within the National Council of Jewish Women. They decided to launch a campaign within their organization that would begin with the grassroots support of their local Essex County division and build a record that could be taken to the national organization.

First, they set up an environmental task force of the 4,300-member Essex County division of the National Council of Jewish Women. The task force undertook a one-year study of food irradiation and sponsored a forum, inviting both proponents and opponents of the process. Even elected officials attending this first forum went home vowing to fight installation of any more irradiators, especially in their own backyards. Their concerns were also aired on local cable television shows.

In April 1986, the National Council of Jewish Women formed a coalition, the Women's Environmental Consortium of New Jersey, with the Junior Leagues of New Jersey and the American Association of University Women (AAUW), to create a broader forum on issues of particular interest to women. Based on the one-year study conducted by the National Council on Jewish Women, food irradiation became the first forum topic. More than 500 leaders from government, religion, education, industry, civic organizations, and the press were invited to participate in a forum on November 18, 1986, presenting arguments for and against food irradiation, and 101 attended. The issue will soon be presented to the national organization.

Consumers United for Food Safety (CUFFS) was formed by concerned citizens in the state of Washington after the FDA-proposed rule alerted them to the possibility that irradiation would be applied to foods. CUFFS members researched the food irradiation issue and prepared educational materials to inform the public. Then they turned to key organizations in the area, approaching them to pass resolutions opposing food irradiation without further research and demanding honest consumer labeling on any allowed irradiated foods. The Group Health Cooperative of Puget Sound, with 330,000 members, adopted such resolutions on April 27, 1985, and the Puget Sound Cooperative Federation (whose members include many food co-ops) adopted two resolutions on August 19, 1985.[33]

## What Can You Do?

As citizen activists, you can circulate petitions, a basic organizing tool of any political campaign. For a model petition see Appendix 6. You can write articles for organization newsletters, introduce resolutions at organization meetings, and organize forums and other educational events. You can utilize printed materials from national or local groups, as long as such materials are not copyrighted or they are otherwise dedicated to public use, tailoring the information to meet the needs of your organization. Citizens can form a new group to focus on food irradiation and related issues, or raise food irradiation concerns in existing organizations like those mentioned earlier.

Acting with some of the local and national organizations working on this issue, you can do these things:


- Contact the NCSFI for information on local organizing.
- Use the model petition in Appendix 6 and write letters to gather support for the campaign to halt food irradiation until the issues of concern have been properly addressed.
- Organize seminars, forums, and public meetings. The case for concern is a strong one; that of the pro-irradiation lobby is weak, so we should not be afraid to organize debates where their case can be challenged.
- Introduce resolutions at meetings of community organizations, labor unions, and national bodies.

- Write to your elected representatives at the local, state, and federal levels. Urge them to support existing bills calling for a halt to irradiation and to put forward new legislation to control the process, guarantee further study, and protect consumers' rights.
- Support national legislation by coordinating petitions, letters, phone calls, and visits to members of Congress.

## International Campaigning

It is also important that we recognize the international nature of this issue. As we have shown, there is much that can be learned from other countries, just as we have learned much from each other and the many researchers around the world who have helped to uncover information on the real risks and benefits of irradiation. In the list of contacts in Appendix 5, we include some of the key national contacts for some of these other countries. The list is necessarily incomplete. The network is growing rapidly. Your information on successes, lessons learned from success or failure, and the information you uncover will help this international movement to grow.

Within Europe, such international coordination has already produced results. Despite permits for irradiation in all European countries but West Germany and Britain, the European Parliament voted on March 10, 1987, to

- Reject general authorization of food irradiation on precautionary grounds.
- Insist that before it is used EEC-wide there be a method of detecting whether a food has been irradiated.
- Insist that there be mandatory labeling of all irradiated foods.
- Call on the European Commission to study alternative methods of preserving food for the countries that have already approved it.
- Call for a ban on imports of irradiated food and animal feed from non-EEC member states.[34]

With the growing international trade (and trade conflicts) between the United States and Europe, this becomes an important consideration for American companies thinking of using the process for the export trade.

There is also potential conflict between the United States and Canada on this issue. A recent report to the Canadian government recommended that the whole issue needed further study before general clearances could be given for irradiation.[35]

This book has attempted to provide some of the facts and to identify some of the pressures for and against the irradiation of food. In doing so, we may have pleased no one, as we have not taken a position that is totally opposed to irradiation under all circumstances. At the same time, we have been highly critical of many of the arguments used in favor of the technology.

We believe that it is now up to the public to make its feelings known on this issue. The debate has moved beyond the closed realm of scientific experts and those with vested interests. It is now a public issue. But, as we have shown, powerful forces are seeking to extend its use in the United States and to gain international acceptance by those countries that have so far retained a ban on its use.

Consumer acceptance or rejection of irradiated foods may influence the scale of involvement of the food trade, but will not of itself halt the use of irradiation, guarantee consumers' rights, or bring to light the hidden pressures and motives for the hasty development of the process. Only coordinated local and national campaigns involving a broad coalition of interests—not all of whom will have the same concerns—can bring about the moratorium on further developments and the public review of all the risks and benefits that is now urgently needed.

---

REFERENCES

1. American Medical Association policy statement, 1986.
2. Irradiation of Foodstuffs. British Medical Association Board of Science, London, March 1987.
3. Keith Schaefer. Conversation with Joe Coleman, DOE Byproduct and Utilization Program, February 18, 1987.
4. Keith Schaefer. Telephone call to NRC, Washington, DC, February 17, 1987.
5. Health and Human Services NEWS press release, Washington, DC, December 12, 1985.
6. 51 Federal Register 13376, 13398, 13399, April 18, 1986.

7. Bill No. S 263 in State of Vermont Senate amending Sec. 16 VSA Chapter 22 to establish Section 201, Labeling of Irradiated Foods 1986.

8. California Senate Joint Resolution 58, adopted August 28, 1986.

9. Legislative Document No. 1552 (1987) An Act to Prohibit Sale of Foods Processed with Radiation, State of Maine.

10. Bill No. S 2571 in the New Jersey Senate and Bill No. A 3150 in State of New Jersey Assembly 202nd Legislature, 1986-87; Mark Magyar. Irradiation Ban Clears Senate. *Bergen Record* (New Jersey), February 2, 1987.

11. For details, contact NCSFI, see Appendix 5 for address.

12. *Milwaukee Journal*, December 5, 1986; January 17, 1987.

13. *Milwaukee Journal*, January 17, 1987.

14. Tony Webb and Tim Lang. Food Irradiation—The Facts. London: Thorsons, 1987.

15. Sharon Bomer, Chairperson, Coalition for Food Irradiation. Letter to James C. Miller, OMB, February 13, 1986.

16. Marie McDermott, Manager, Thomas J. Lipton, Inc. Letter to Betsy Russ, November 5, 1986.

17. *Citizens Against Irradiated Food Newsletter.* 27 State St., Norwalk, Ohio 44857, December 1986.

18. Letter to Betsy Russ from Dale Arett, dated October 28, 1986.

19. Statement from George Giddings of Isomedix made in Boston, October 21, 1986, to K. Tucker.

20. *Wall Street Journal*, March 31, 1987, Section 2. p. 1.

21. Letter from Santa Rosa Community Foods, dated April 11, 1984, sent to FDA.

22. Letter from Thomas F. Burns, Executive Vice President of American Spice Trade Association to FDA, dated April 13, 1984.

23. Letter from Robert K. Curtis, Research Coordinator. Almond Board of California, dated April 21, 1984.

24. Robert N. Turner, Washington State Apple Commission. Letter to FDA, April 2, 1984.

25. B. L. Mitchell, Division of Regulatory Guidance, Center for Food Safety and Applied Nutrition. Letter to Connie Wheeler (CUFFS), June 26, 1986.

26. John C. Datt, American Farm Bureau Federation. Letter to FDA, April 16, 1984.

27. 1982—Year of Breakthroughs: Industry Vows to Make Pork Trichina Safe by 1987. *Pork Challenger,* March 1983. Hearings on H. R. 2496, Procurement and Military Nuclear Systems Subcommittee of the House Committee on Armed Military Nuclear Services, 98th Congress 1st Session, March 1-2, 1983, pp. 207-208.

28. Denis Mosgofian. Lookin' for a Home...Justa Lookin' for a Home...: Food Irradiation: An Atoms-for-Peace Orphan; the 1950s Revisited. National Coalition to Stop Food Irradiation, 1986.

29. Debbie Berkowitz, Health and Safety Director, Food and Allied Service Trades, Department of AFL-CIO. Statement to London Food Commission. Washington, DC, March 1987.

30. ECF Position on Document Com (85) 603 final of the EC, November 1985, Completion of the Internal Market: Community Legislation on Foodstuffs; European Committee of Food Catering and Allied Workers Unions within the International Union of Foodworkers (ECF-IUF), Brussels, June 12, 1986.

31. Oppose Food Irradiation: Resolution No. 17 Presented by Graphic Communications, No. 583, San Francisco, to the California Labor Federation, AFL-CIO, Sacramento, July 1986.

32. *Marketing Guidelines for Acceptance and Usage of Food Irradiation.* Task Force on Marketing and Public Relations of the International Consultative group on Food Irradiation (ICGFI), Vienna, September 15-19, 1986.

33. Press release from Consumers United for Food Safety. Group Health Membership Votes to Oppose Food Irradiation (Resolution adopted April 27, 1985), May 1, 1985. Letter from Carol Bergin, Co-Director of Puget Sound Cooperative Federation to HEI, with attached resolutions adopted August 19, 1985, (September 12, 1985).

34. Opinion of the European Parliament on Irradiation of Foodstuffs, Brussels, adopted April 10, 1987.

35. Report of the Standing Committee on Consumer and Corporate Affairs on the subject of food irradiation and the labeling of irradiated foods. House of Commons, Ottawa, Canada, 1987.

# UNITED STATES LICENSED GAMMA IRRADIATION FACILITIES

| Company | Location |
| --- | --- |
| Abbott Laboratories | North Chicago, IL |
| Agriculture, Department of | Beltsville, MD |
| Air Force, Department of | Brooks AFB, TX |
| | Hanscom AFB, MA |
| Akron, University of | Akron, OH |
| American Pharmaseal Co. | El Paso, TX |
| (Baxter Travenol) | Irwindale, CA |
| Applied Radiant Energy Corp. | Lynchburg, VA* |
| Army, Department of | Adelphi, MD |
| | Dover, NJ |
| | Fort Monmouth, NJ |
| | Natick, MA |
| | Washington, DC |
| | White Sands, NM |
| Baxter Travenol | Puerto Rico |
| Becton-Dickenson | Broken Bow, NE |
| | North Canaan, CT |
| | Sumter, SC |
| Brandeis University | Waltham, MA |
| Central Serv. Org., Inc. | Morristown, NJ |
| Cincinnati, University of | Cincinnati, OH |
| Cobe Laboratories | Lakewood, CO |
| Commerce, Department of | Gloucester, MA |
| | Washington, DC |
| Defense Nuclear Agency | Bethesda, MD |
| Dow Corning Corp. | Midland, MI (2 licenses) |
| Ethicon, Inc. | San Angelo, TX |
| (Johnson & Johnson) | Somerville, NJ |
| General Electric Co. | Philadelphia, PA |
| General Foods Corp. | Cranbury, NJ |
| Goodyear Tire & Rubber | Akron, OH |

| Company | Location |
| --- | --- |
| Gulf Research & Development Co. | Cambridge, MA |
| Harvard University | Cambridge, MA |
| Hawaii, University of | Honolulu, HI |
| Health & Human Services | Atlanta, GA |
| IBM Corp. | Manassas, VA |
| Illinois, University of | Chicago, IL |
| Indiana State University | Terre Haute, IN |
| International Nutronics | Dover, NJ |
| | Palo Alto, CA* |
| | Irvine, CA* |
| Iotech, Inc. | Northglenn, CO |
| Iowa, University of | Ames, IA |
| IRT Corp. | San Diego, CA |
| Isomedix, Inc. | Columbus, MS* |
| | Groveport, OH |
| | Libertyville, IL* |
| | Morton Grove, IL* |
| | Northborough, MA* |
| | Parsippany, NJ |
| | Sandy, UT* |
| | Spartanburg, SC* |
| | Vega Alta, PR* |
| | Whippany, NJ (6 licenses) |
| Jackson Laboratories | Bar Harbor, ME |
| Johnson & Johnson | New Brunswick, NJ |
| | Sherman, TX |
| Meloy Laboratories, Inc. | Springfield, VA |
| Merck & Co. | West Point, PA |
| Minnesota Mining & | Brookings, SD |
| Manufacturing Co. | St. Paul, MN |
| Minnesota, University of | Minneapolis, MN |
| Missouri, University of | Columbia, MO |
| National Aeronautics & | Green Belt, MD |
| Space Administration | Moffett, CA |
| Navy, Department of | Crane, IN |
| Neutron Products | Dickerson, MD (2 licenses)* |
| Pennsylvania State University | University Park, PA |
| Permagrain Products | Media, PA |
| Precision Materials Corp. | Mine Hill, NJ |

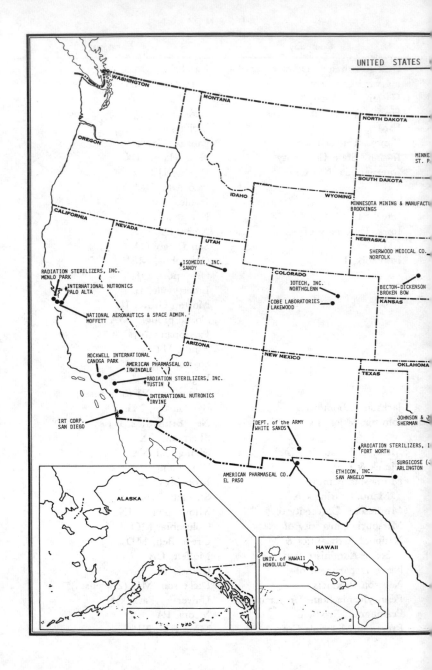

UNITED STATES

WASHINGTON

MONTANA

OREGON

NORTH DAKOTA

MINNE
ST. P

IDAHO

SOUTH DAKOTA

WYOMING

CALIFORNIA

NEVADA

UTAH

MINNESOTA MINING & MANUFACTU
BROOKINGS

NEBRASKA

ISOMEDIX INC.
SANDY

SHERWOOD MEDICAL CO.
NORFOLK

RADIATION STERILIZERS, INC.
MENLO PARK

COLORADO

IOTECH, INC.
NORTHGLENN

BECTON-DICKENSON
BROKEN BOW

INTERNATIONAL NUTRONICS
PALO ALTA

COBE LABORATORIES
LAKEWOOD

KANSAS

NATIONAL AERONAUTICS & SPACE ADMIN.
MOFFETT

ARIZONA

NEW MEXICO

OKLAHOMA

ROCKWELL INTERNATIONAL
CANOGA PARK

AMERICAN PHARMASEAL CO.
IRWINDALE

TEXAS

RADIATION STERILIZERS, INC.
TUSTIN

JOHNSON & J
SHERMAN

INTERNATIONAL NUTRONICS
IRVINE

IRT CORP.
SAN DIEGO

DEPT. of the ARMY
WHITE SANDS

RADIATION STERILIZERS, I
FORT WORTH

SURGICOSE (
ARLINGTON

AMERICAN PHARMASEAL CO.
EL PASO

ETHICON, INC.
SAN ANGELO

ALASKA

HAWAII

UNIV. of HAWAII
HONOLULU

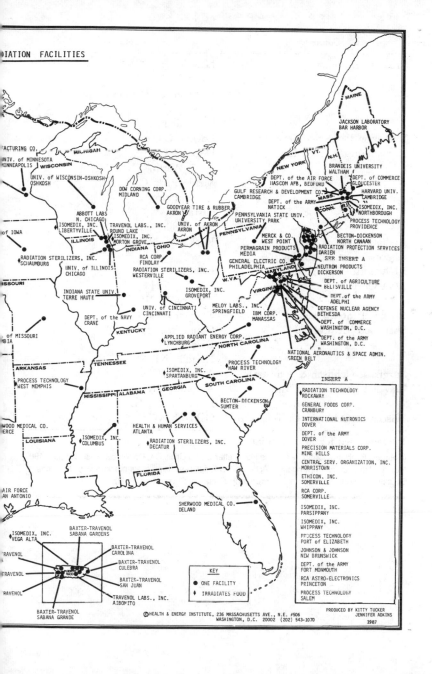

IATION FACILITIES

| Company | Location |
| --- | --- |
| Process Technology | Haw River, NC* |
| | Port of Elizabeth, NJ |
| | Providence, RI (Design phase) |
| | Salem, NJ |
| | West Memphis, AR* |
| Radiation Protection Services | Darien, CT |
| Radiation Sterilizers, Inc. | Decatur, GA* |
| | Forth Worth, TX* |
| | Menlo Park, CA |
| | Schaumburg, IL* |
| | Tustin, CA* |
| | Westerville, OH |
| Radiation Technology (see Process Technology) | Rockaway, NJ* |
| RCA Astro-Electronics | Princeton, NJ |
| RCA Corp. | Findlay, OH |
| | Somerville, NJ |
| Rockwell International | Canoga Park, CA |
| Sherwood Medical Co. | Commerce, TX |
| | Deland, FL |
| | Norfolk, NE |
| Surgikose (Johnson & Johnson) | Arlington, TX |
| Travenol Laboratories, Inc. | Aibonito, PR |
| | Round Lake, IL |
| Wisconsin-Oshkosh, University of | Oshkosh, WI |

*already used for food irradiation

(Sources: Food Irradiation Response Newsletter. Santa Cruz, CA, December 1986/January 1987. Nuclear Regulatory Commission. Active NRC Licenses—Irradiators other > 10,000 curies, September 1986. NRC In-house Irradiation Facilities, September 1986.)

# U.K. HOUSE OF COMMONS MOTIONS ON IRRADIATED FOODS

### Notices of Questions and Motions: 9th April 1986

**713** IRRADIATED FOOD: CONFLICT OF INTEREST

Mr Dennis Skinner
Mr Tony Lloyd
Mr Richard Caborn
Mr Brian Sedgemore
Mr Robert Litherland
Mr Ernie Ross

That this House expresses concern about conflict of interest between the work of Her Majesty's Government's Advisory Committee on Irradiated and Novel Foods and the changing position of companies who stand to benefit from its recommendations: notes that the predictions of the main recommendation of the Committee, that the current ban on irradiated food can be lifted, have been widely leaked, not least by Mr Frank Ley, the Committee's technical and economic adviser; notes that Mr Ley is the Marketing Director of ISOTRON, a company which is in a semi-monopolistic position to take advantage of a change in law allowing food to be irradiated in Britain; notes that while the Committee sat, ISOTRON, despite its existing production overcapacity, commissioned a new plant and raised capital through a flotation on the Stock Exchange; notes the rise in ISOTRON's capital value when the financial press linked the future of the company to the impending recommendations of the Advisory Committee; believes that Mr Ley's high public profile, designed to help ISOTRON financially, was incompatible with his role as regards the Advisory Committee; calls on all the directors of ISOTRON to give an account of their share interests and charges on them since flotation; and calls on Her Majesty's Government to make a statement and the Stock Exchange to carry out an investigation, so as to satisfy themselves that nothing improper has occurred.

**714** IRRADIATED FOOD: ILLEGAL IMPORTATION

Mr Frank Cook
Mr Richard Caborn
Mr Robert Litherland
Mr Ernie Ross
Mr Brian Sedgemore
Mr Tony Lloyd

That this House notes with grave concern the admission of a company from the Imperial Food Group that, having had a consignment of prawns condemned by the Southampton Port Health Authority on the grounds of bacterial contamination, it had the consignment irradiated by Gammaster B.Y. in the Netherlands to conceal such bacterial contamination and caused them to be reimported; notes that this practice is illegal under the United Kingdom Food (Control of Irradiation) Regulations; notes too that it is also contrary to the recommendations of the Joint Export Committee of the World Health Organization Food and Agriculture Organization of the United Nations and the International Atomic Energy Agency, which bodies demand that irradiation be used solely to extend the shelf life of food otherwise wholesome and never be used to conceal contamination, thereby rendering saleable food that is not truly wholesome, notes further that this instance highlights the inadequacy of existing food monitoring provisions and standards of enforcement procedures, presenting a potential public health hazard; calls on the Imperial Food Group to give to their shareholders, and to the shareholders of United Biscuits, a full explanation of how and why they became involved in such a scandalous practice; requires them to give, too, a public undertaking that such a major misdemeanor will not be repeated, calls upon Her Majesty's Government to alert all port health and trading standards authorities to the possible prospect of such malpractice; and finally urges the Director of Public Prosecutions to investigate these matters fully with a view to initiating appropriate legal proceedings against the offending company.

---

**715  IRRADIATED FOOD: SAFETY AND WHOLESOMENESS**
Mr Frank Cook
Mr Robert Litherland
Mr Tony Lloyd
Mr Richard Caborn
Mr Ernie Ross
Mr Brian Sedgemore

| | | |
|---|---|---|
| Mr Stan Thorne | Miss Joan Maynard | Mr Allen McKay |
| Mr George Park | Mr Bob Clay | Mr Lewis Carter-Jones |
| Mr Laurie Pavitt | Mr Sean Hughes | |

That this House, in welcoming the publication of the report of the Advisory Committee on Irradiated and Novel Foods, draws to the attention of Her Majesty's Government: (a) the public concern over reports in the scientific literature of lowered birth rates, lower growth rates and kidney damage in some experimental animals fed on irradiated diets and the incidence of polyploidy, a chromosomal defect, in children and animals fed on freshly irradiated wheat, (b) the severe loss of vitamins caused in some foods by irradiation and the possible effect this may have on people who, as a result of low income levels, are on a diet already inadequate, (c) the inadequacy of the current Ionising Radiation Regulatory Requirements for the protection of workers in irradiation plants, (d) the possible abuse of irradiation to conceal bacterial contamination of food, whilst leaving unaffected those toxins that may have been created by bacterial contamination at an earlier stage of handling or processing, (e) the absence of adequate methods or systems for testing for such hazards to public health by the port health and trading standards authorities, the only public bodies charged with responsibility in regard to these matters, and (f) the clear need for consumers to have all irradiated food unmistakably labeled as such at the point of sale, whether sold loose, packaged, in bulk, or through catering outlets for consumption on or off the premises.

Daily Mail, Monday, March 3, 1986

# We broke law with gamma ray prawns says food firm

**By STEPHEN LEATHER, Consumer Affairs Correspondent**

ONE of Britain's biggest food groups has sold radiation-treated prawns in contravention of health regulations.

The Imperial Group admits it broke the law last year after a consignment of prawns from Malaysia failed quality-control tests.

Instead of scrapping the seafood, it was shipped to Holland, sterilised with gamma radiation and then brought back and sold under the Admiral label to caterers.

Imperial Group — its products include Courage beer, Ross frozen foods, Golden Wonder and Young's Seafoods — said : 'In January 1935 we bought two containers of Malaysian warm water prawns. They were imported through Southampton, where they were tested by the health authorities. Then they went into public cold store.

'In February we took them out. We didn't have to test them again, but we did. We tested 46 batches. Twenty passed but 26 did not — our standards for these tests are very nigh.

'There was nothing to stop us selling the prawns because they had been passed by the health authorities — but our standards are higher. The decision was taken to send them to Holland for irradiation. Holland is a world leader in this type of treatment.'

A certificate shows the Dutch firm of Gammaster treated three batches of cooked, peeled prawns in April. They were then returned to Britain.

The spokesman said that by the end of May, all the radiation-treated prawns had been sold, mainly to Indian restaurants and caterers.

The Department of Health confirmed that it is illegal to sell irradiated food in Britain and that the trading standards office at the port of entry would be investigating.

Prosecution could result in a fine of up to £2,000 or three months' jail.

Irradiation is widely used to sterilise food in Europe and America — there is no evidence that treated food is unsafe. The treatment allows it to be kept for much longer, which can reduce its nutritional value.

CERTIFICATE OF GAMMA IRRADIATION No. 214
-----------------------------------------

This is to certify that :

GAMMASTER B.V. - Ede - Holland

has given an irradiation treatment
to the following goods :

CUSTOMER :              Young's Seafoods Ltd., London,

PRODUCT :               Bulk IQF cooked & peeled prawns 300/400

QUANTITY :              1. 1278 x 38 lbs
                        2. 180 x 38 lbs and 572 x 25 lbs

CHARGENUMBER :          1. 850423
                        2. 850423-24/NW5-029

IRRADIATION DATE :      1. 23-04-1985
                        2. 23/24-04-1985

IRRADIATION MODE :      JS 9000 IRRADIATOR

IRRADIATION DOSE :      3 kGy

                                        GAMMASTER B.V.
                                        Ede   - Holland


Acc. Controller :



Acc. Plant Manager :

# RESPONSE TO U.S. SURVEY

| Manufacturer | Irradiating | Irradiated Ingredients | Conducts Research | Concept |
|---|---|---|---|---|
| Armour-Dial Corp. | No | No | No | No |
| Beatrice-Hunt/ Wesson | No | Yes-Spices | Interested in | technology |
| Best Foods (Hellman's, Mazola Skippy) | No | No | No | DNA |
| Bordens | No | No | No | No |
| Campbell's Soup Company | No | DNA | DNA | Yes-Coalition |
| Carnation | No | No | Yes | believes promising |
| Celestial Seasonings | DNA | No | DNA | DNA |
| Chelsea Milling Co. (Jiffy Mixes) | No | No | No | No |
| Compass Foods (8 o'clock bean coffee) | | No | No | No |
| Dannon Company, Inc. | DNA | No | DNA | DNA |
| Fearn Natural Foods | No | No | No | No |
| R.T. French Co. (French's) | DNA | No | Irradiation has potential | |
| Gorton's Fish | No | No | No plans to irr. in future | |
| Hartville Kitchen (salad dressings) | DNA | No | DNA | DNA |
| Heinz | No | DNA | Yes | DNA |
| Hollywood Foods | No | No | DNA | DNA |
| Holsum Foods | No | DNA | No | thinks safe |
| Hormel | No | No | DNA | DNA |
| I&K Dist., Inc. | No | No | No | No |
| Lawsons Company (dairy products) | No | No | DNA | DNA |
| The Larsen Company (Freshlike Veg.) | No | No | Evaluating concept | |
| Thomas J. Lipton, Inc. | No | DNA | No | Yes-Coalition |
| Miami Margarine Co. | No | No | No | DNA |

| Manufacturer | Irradiating | Irradiated Ingredients | Conducts Research | Concept |
|---|---|---|---|---|
| Miss Molly Foods | | | | |
| (TV dinners) | No | No | DNA | DNA |
| Nature's Plus | | | | |
| (vitamins) | No | No | No | No |
| Nature's Way | | | | |
| (herbal powders) | No | No | DNA | DNA |
| Nestle Foods | No | No | No position | No position |
| Ocean Spray | | | | |
| Cranberries, Inc. | No | No | No | No position |
| Oscar-Mayer | No | No | DNA | DNA |
| Ralston-Purina (human | | | | |
| and pet foods) | No | No | No | Believes safe |
| J.H. Routh Packaging | | | | |
| (pork products) | No | No | DNA | DNA |
| Swift-Eckrich | DNA | DNA | Are evaluating concept | |
| Starkist Foods, Inc. | | | | |
| (human and | | | | |
| pet foods) | No | No | DNA | DNA |
| Sunny Delight Juices | No | No | No | DNA |
| Weaver Foods | No | No | No | DNA |
| **SPICES:** | | | | |
| Durkee Famous Foods | No | - | - | - |
| Kroger | No | - | - | - |
| McCormick | not retail | - | Yes | - |
| Mrs. Dash | | | | |
| (Alberto-Culver) | No | DNA | DNA | DNA |
| Topco (Food Club | | | | |
| Spices) | No | - | - | - |
| Ragu products do not | | | | |
| contain irradiated | | | | |
| herbs or spices. | | | | |
| **BABY FOOD:** | | | | |
| Beech-Nut | No | No | No | No |
| Gerber | No | No | Yes | - |
| Heinz | No | - | - | - |

DNA, did not answer.
From C.A.IR. Newsletter, December 1986.

## Sample Letter to Food Processors

If you want to help or if you're at a loss for words, the letter below will get you started.

Every food label contains the manufacturer's name, city, state and zip code. That's all the post office needs to forward your letter. Always flag the outside of the envelope with the words "ATTN: Consumer Inquiry." It will be helpful to become familiar with the corporate name as well as the product name. For example, when you say "Wishbone Salad Dressings" you might think that "Wishbone" is the company's name, when closer scrutiny of the label will reveal Thomas J. Lipton, Inc., as the manufacturer.

Dear Sir or Madam:

As a consumer of your company's fine products, I would like to know if they have been irradiated, or if they contain irradiated ingredients.

Could you also tell me if you are conducting test research on irradiated food or promoting the concept of food irradiation.

So that I may continue to make informed decisions at the grocery store, I hope to hear from you soon.

Sincerely,

# CONGRESSMAN DOUGLAS BOSCOE'S BILL

## A Bill

To prohibit the implementation of certain regulations of the Secretary of Health and Human Services and the Secretary of Agriculture respecting irradiated foods, to amend the Federal Food, Drug and Cosmetic Act to prescribe labels for irradiated food, and for other purposes.

Be it enacted by the Senate and House of Representatives of the United States of America in Congress assembled,

### Section 1. Short Title

This Act may be cited as the "Food Irradiation Safety and Labeling Requirement Act of 1987."

### Section 2. Regulations

(a) IRRADIATION OF PORK: The Secretary of Agriculture may not implement the regulations relating to the irradiation of pork published in 51 Federal Register 1769 and may not issue any other regulation which would have the same legal effect as such regulations. The Secretary of Health and Human Services may not implement the regulations relating to the irradiation of pork published in 50 Federal Register 29658 and may not issue any other regulation which would have the same legal effect as such regulations.

(b) IRRADIATION OF OTHER FOODS: The Secretary of Health and Human Services may not implement the regulations relating to the irradiation of food published in 51 Federal Register 13376. The Secretary may not issue any other regulation which would have the same legal effect as such regulations.

### Section 3. Study

(a) GENERAL RULE: The Secretary of Health and Human Services shall arrange, in accordance with subsection (b), for a study of the risk to human health and the environment presented by the irradiation of food. The study shall include the following:

(1) A review of existing research on the safety and wholesomeness of consumption of irradiated food and the conduct of new studies on the consumption and nutritional value of irradiated food.

(2) A study of the contamination of food from improper radiation.

(3) A study of the risk to the health of individuals employed in facilities in which irradiation is conducted and an evaluation of the exposure to radiation, emergency medical plans for radiation accidents or emergencies, safety requirements in effect in such facilities, and employee training in safe irradiation procedures.

(4) A study of the risk to the health of residents of the area in which such facilities are located which may result from the accidental release from such facilities of the source of the food irradiation and an evaluation of the existing technology for cleaning such facilities when there has been an accidental release within the facility, methods for the evacuation of such areas in the case of such a release, emergency response systems, and an identification of persons responsible for cleaning facilities and personal liability for accidental releases.

(5) A study of the effect on the environment, on population centers of over 50,000, and rural areas of transporting the sources of food irradiation and the protection of the drivers and the general public from injury from such transportation and an identification of the persons responsible for personal liability for accidents in transporting such sources.

(b) ARRANGEMENT: The Secretary shall arrange with the National Academy of Sciences to conduct the study prescribed by Subsection (a) or, if such an arrangement cannot be entered into, with another nonprofit private research entity with appropriate qualifications.

(c) REPORT: The Secretary shall report the results of the study not later than 2 years after the date of the enactment of this Act.

## Section 4. Labeling Requirement

Section 403 of the Federal Food, Drug, and Cosmetic Act (21 U.S.C. 343) is amended by adding at the end the following:

"(q)(1)(A) If it is a food which has been treated with ionizing or gamma radiation unless the food is labeled or marked—

"(i) to provide notice that the food has received ionizing or gamma radiation or if it is composed of ingredients which have received such radiation, that the ingredients of the food have received such radiation, and

"(ii) to warn that the food should not be subject to further radiation.

"(B) The Secretary shall issue regulations respecting the labeling required by clause (A). Such regulations shall

"(i) require that the labels appear in a conspicuous place on food retail and wholesale packages,

"(ii) in the case of non-packaged foods, require that the contents of the label be placed in the notice displayed prominently where such food is held for sale, and "(iii) require that the label statement appear in any invoice accompanying the food.

"(2) If it is a food which has been treated with ionizing or gamma radiation and which is offered for sale in a restaurant unless it has a mark placed beside it in the restaurant's menu with the explanation that the mark means that the food has been treated with ionizing or gamma radiation.

"(3) Any person engaged in the irradiation of food shall report semiannually to the Secretary—

"(A) a summary of all the foods that the person irradiated in the period reported on,

"(B) the categories of food irradiated and the total amount of food in each such category which was irradiated,

"(C) the persons for whom the irradiation was done and the types and amount of food irradiated for such persons,

"(D) the dosage levels of irradiation for each category of food irradiated and the method of calculating the dosage levels, and

"(E) assurances that its irradiation procedures are established by experts qualified in radiation processing of food.

The Secretary shall make such reports available to the public and may not destroy any such report."

*Section 5. Exports*

Section 801 (d) (1) of the Federal Food, Drug and Cosmetic Act (21 U.S.C. 381 (d) (1)) is amended by striking out "and" at the end of subparagraph (C), by redesignating subparagraph (D) as subparagraph (E), and by inserting after subparagraph (C) the following:

"(D) is a food which has been treated with ionizing or gamma radiation and is labeled in accordance with section 403 (q)(1) and does not bear or contain any food additive which is unsafe within the meaning of section 409, and..."

*Section 6. Enforcement*

Section 301 of the Federal Food, Drug and Cosmetic Act (21 U.S.C. 331) is amended by adding at the end the following:

"(t) The failure to make the report required by section 403(q) (3)".

*Section 7. Effective Date*

The amendments made by sections 4, 5 and 6 shall take effect upon the expiration of 180 days after the date of the enactment of this Act.

House Resolution 956
100th Congress 1st Session

# Co-Sponsors to H.R. 956

*Original:*

1. Peter Rodino (D, N.J.)
2. Matthew Rinaldo (R, N.J.)
3. Robert Mrazek (D, N.Y.)
4. Robert Roe (D, N.J.)
5. Edward Feighan (D, Ohio)
6. Walter Fauntroy (D, D.C.)
7. Antony Beilenson (D, Calif.)
8. Bob Kastenmeier (D, Wisc.)
9. Frank Annunzio (D, Ill.)
10. Ben Gilman (R, N.Y.)
11. Mario Biaggi (D, N.Y.)
12. Ron Dellums (D, Calif.)
13. Major Owens (D, N.Y.)
14. Jim Howard (D, N.J.)
15. Leon Panetta (D, Calif.)
16. Andrew Jacobs (D, Ind.)
17. Frank Guarini (D, N.J.)
18. Barbara Boxer (D, Calif.)
19. Gary Ackerman (D, N.Y.)
20. Olympia Snowe (R, Ma.)
21. Pete Stark (D, Calif.)
22. Glenn Anderson (D, Calif.)
23. Peter Kostmayer (D, Penn.)
24. Ted Weiss (D, N.Y.)
25. William Lipinski (D, Ill.)
26. John Conyers (D, Mich.)
27. Sam Gejdenson (D, Conn.)
28. Stephen Solarz (D, N.Y.)
29. Mike Lowry (D, Wash.)
30. Dean Gallo (R, N.J.)
31. Barbara Kennelly (D, Conn.)
32. Charles Schumer (D, N.Y.)
33. Claudine Schneider (R, R.I.)
34. Larry Smith (D, Fla.)
35. Walter Jones (D, N.C.)
36. Austin Murphy (D, Penn.)
37. Don Sundquist (R, Tenn.)
38. Charles Hayes (D, Ill.)
39. Robert Borski (D, Penn.)
40. Bill Richardson (D, N.M.)
41. Albert Bustamante (D, Tex.)
42. Esteban Torres (D, Calif.)
43. Peter DeFazio (D, Oreg.)
44. Ed Towns (D, N.Y.)
45. Robert Garcia (D, N.Y.)
46. Joe Kolter (D, Penn.)
47. Kenneth Gray (D, Ill.)
48. Edward Boland (D, Ill.)
49. Augustus Hawkins (D, Calif.)
50. George (Buddy) Darden (D, Ga.)

*Additional Co-sponsors:*

51. James Florio (D, N.J.)
52. Chris Smith (R, N.J.)
53. Nicholas Mavroules (D, Mass.)
54. James Mavroules (D, Ohio)
55. Silvio Conte (R, Mass.)
56. Howard Berman (D, Calif.)
57. Robert Roe (D, N.J.)
58. Jim Courter (R, N.J.)
59. Pat Schroeder (D, Colo.)
60. Chester Atkins (D, Mass.)
61. Jim Saxton (R, N.J.)
62. Joe Kennedy (D, Mass.)
63. Ed Markey (D, Mass.)
64. George Crockett (D, Mich.)
65. Jim Moody (D, Wisc.)
66. Louis Stokes (D, Ohio)
67. Tom Lantos (D, Calif.)
68. Louise Slaugher (D, N.Y.)

# CONTACTS AND ADDRESSES

*U.S. Congress*

Senators
The US Senate
Washington, DC 20510

Congressional Representatives
The US House of Representatives
Washington, DC 20515

*Administrative Agencies*

Food & Drug Administration
5600 Fishers Lane
Rockville, MD 20857

US Department of Agriculture
14th and Independence Avenue SW
Washington, DC 20250

Nuclear Regulatory Commission
Washington, DC 20553

*U.S. Contacts*

Americans for Safe Food
P.O. Box 66300
Washington, DC 20035
*contact:* Dr. Michael Jacobson

National Coalition to Stop Food
  Irradiation (NCSFI)
P.O. Box 590488
San Francisco, CA 94159
USA
*contact:* Denis Mosgofian

Health & Energy Institute
Suite 506
236 Massachusetts Ave NE
Washington, DC 20002
USA
*contact:* Kitty Tucker

People for Responsible Management
  of Radioactive Waste
3 Whitman Drive
Denville, NJ 07834
USA
*contact:* Dr. Wally Burnstein

Food and Water, Inc.
(same as above)

Public Citizen Health
  Research Group
2000 P Street NW
Washington, DC 20036
USA
*contact:* Dr. Sidney Wolfe

Food Irradiation Response Newsletter
Box 5183
Santa Cruz, CA 95063

Consumers United for Food Safety
P.O. Box 22928
Seattle, WA 98122
USA
*contact:* Connie Wheeler

Oregon Coalition to Stop
Food Irradiation
13665 South Mueller
Oregon City, OR 97045
USA
*contact:* Hale Weitzman

Coalition for Alternatives in
Nutrition & Health Care
P.O. Box B-12
Richlandtown, PA 18955
USA
*contact:* Catherine Frompovich, Ph.D.

Food and Allied Service Trades
AFL-CIO
815 16th St. NW, Suite 408
Washington, DC 20006
USA
*contact:* Debbie Berkowitz

Coalition For Food Irradiation
NFPA, Suite 900
605 14th Street NW
Washington, DC 20005
*contact:* Ellen Green

\* for other local groups contact
NCSFI above

*Canada*

Pollution Probe Foundation
12 Madison Avenue
Toronto M5R 2S1
Canada
*contacts:* Linda Pim and David Poch

International Institute of Concern
for Public Health
Suite 343, 67 Mowat Avenue
Toronto M6K 3E3
Canada

Consumers United to Stop
Food Irradiation
R.R. #1
Ilderton, Ontario N0M 2A0
Canada
*contact:* Ann Marie Brown

Standing Committee on
Corporate and Consumer
Affairs on Food Irradiation
House of Commons
Ottawa, Canada
*contact:* Mary Collins, MP
(Chairperson)

*International Contacts*

International Organisation of
Consumer Unions (IOCU)
Regional Office for Asia and
the Pacific
P.O. Box 1045
10830 Penang
Malaysia
*contact:* Dr. Martin Abraham

IOCU (Europe)
Ammastraat G
2595 Eb Den Haag
The Netherlands
*contact:* Atie Schipaanboord

In the U.S. contact IOCU UN
representative Esther Peterson

*Britain*

The London Food Commission
88 Old Street
London ECIV 9AR
U.K.
*contact:* Dr. Tim Lang and
Tony Webb

## West Germany

Die Verbraucher Initiative
P.O. Box 1746
D5300 Bonn 1
Federal Republic of Germany
*contact:* Gerd Billen-Girmscheid

Die Grunen
c/o European Parliament
97-113 Rue Balliard
Brussels
1040 Belgium
*contact:* Ulrike Bloch von
    Blotnitz, M.E.P.

## The Netherlands

Konsumentenbond
Leeghwaterplein 26
2521 CV Den Haag
The Netherlands
*contact:* Cor Verhülsolonk

Konsumenten Kontact
P.O. Box 30500
Sweelinckplein 74
2517 GS's-Gravenhage
The Netherlands
*contact:* Marcel Schutterlaar

## Denmark

Noah
Studiestraede 24, St.
DK 1455 Copenhagen K.
Denmark
*contacts:* Jesper Toft

## Finland

Kuluttojat-Konsumenterna Ry
Vilhouk 6-F-31
SF 00100 Helsinki
Finland
*contact:* Gun Vayrynen and
    Heidi Hautala

## Sweden

F.M.K
P.O. Box 8083
S-104 20 Stockholm
Sweden
*contacts:* Aino Blomquist and
    Eia Joss Liljegren

## Australia

John Scott MP
Shops 1 and 2
34 Henley Beach Road
Mile End 3A 5031
Australia

## New Zealand

Friends of the Earth
P.O. Box 38-085
Auckland West
New Zealand
*contact:* Bob Tait

## Japan

Consumers Union of Japan
3-13-29 Nakameguro
Meguro-Ku
Tokyo 153
Japan

*Italy*

Agrisalus
Via Bazzini 24
20131 Milano MI
Italy
*contact:* Andrea Gaifami


These are national contacts who can put you in touch with other, more local initiatives. For an up-to-date list of international contacts, write to the Health and Energy Institute or the London Food Commission.

# FOOD IRRADIATION PETITION

We, the undersigned consumers concerned about the quality of our food, our environment, and our health, petition our government to prevent processing of our foods with ionizing radiation until the safety of the process has been demonstrated for each food, until previous studies showing damaging effects from eating irradiated foods have been replicated, and until all environmental dangers have been assessed. In the event that any food irradiation is allowed, such foods should be required to carry a label that clearly states "treated with ionizing radiation" so that consumers have a choice.

|    | Name (Print legibly) | Address | City/State | Zip | Phone |
|----|----------------------|---------|------------|-----|-------|
| 1. | | | | | |
| 2. | | | | | |
| 3. | | | | | |
| 4. | | | | | |
| 5. | | | | | |
| 6. | | | | | |
| 7. | | | | | |
| 8. | | | | | |
| 9. | | | | | |
| 10.| | | | | |

Please return to: Health & Energy Institute
236 Massachusetts Ave NE, Suite 506
Washington, DC 20002; Phone (202) 543-1070.

# INTERNATIONAL ORGANIZATION OF CONSUMER UNIONS, STATEMENT ON FOOD IRRADIATION

"IOCU's position on food irradiation is to work toward ensuring an informed, participatory and responsible decision-making approach which takes into account many questions which need to be adequately answered, the foremost of which is the real need for it. Two, our concerns about food irradiation include aspects of safety, nutrition, wholesomeness, labeling, control, enforcement, monitoring and, most important, the socioeconomic implications, environmental consequences, dependence creation, and the impact on existing food growing, processing, storage and distribution systems. While there may be some limited, specific and controlled uses for food irradiation under certain strict environmental regimes, we are concerned that the potential benefits have generally been grossly over-rated, while the potential problems have been underplayed. Efforts at adopting misleading, vague and uninformative labeling and attempts to foisting this technology, particularly on the Third World, without the active and informed participation of independent citizens groups must be thwarted."

*(Dr. Martin Abraham, Regional Office for Asia and the Pacific, IOCU, Penang, Malaysia, February 1987)*